Y0-CCA-054

"Why were you at the river after dark?"

"I was..."

"What? Angry at me?"

"Angry at you! Why should I be? All you've told me is how I should be clothed in an apron holding a baby in one arm and stirring the dinner on the stove with the other."

Paulo turned toward her and before she knew it, his arms had encircled her. He was pulling her closer to him. His kiss was fierce at first, bruising her lips into submission; it then became gentle as it deepened into a possession. Her mind whirled with new sensations and a flame of desire ignited deep within her. She melted against his lean, hard frame and returned his kisses...

Dear Reader,

Your enthusiastic reception of SECOND CHANCE AT LOVE has inspired all of us who work on this special romance line and we thank you.

Now there are *six* brand new, exciting SECOND CHANCE AT LOVE romances for you each month. We've doubled the number of love stories in our line because so many readers like you asked us to. So, you see, your opinions, your ideas, what you think, really count! Feel free to drop me a note to let me know your reactions to our stories.

Again, thanks for so warmly welcoming SECOND CHANCE AT LOVE and, please, *do* let me hear from *you*!

With every good wish,

Carolyn Nichols

Carolyn Nichols
SECOND CHANCE AT LOVE
The Berkley/Jove Publishing Group
200 Madison Avenue
New York, New York 10016

P.S. Because your opinions *are* so important to us, I urge you to fill out and return the questionnaire in the back of this book.

Second Chance at Love

GIFT OF ORCHIDS

PATTI MOORE

A
SECOND CHANCE AT LOVE
BOOK

To my husband, Mike.
Without him, this wouldn't
have been possible.

GIFT OF ORCHIDS

Copyright © 1982 by Patti Moore

Distributed by Berkley/Jove

All rights reserved. No part of this publication may be reproduced or transmitted in any form or by any means, electronic or mechanical, including photocopy, recording, or any information storage and retrieval system, without permission in writing from the publisher.

Requests for permission to make copies of any part of the work should be mailed to: Permissions, Second Chance at Love, The Berkley/Jove Publishing Group, 200 Madison Avenue, New York, NY 10016.

First edition published January 1982

First printing

"Second Chance at Love" and the butterfly emblem are trademarks belonging to Jove Publications, Inc.

Printed in the United States of America

Second Chance at Love books are published by
The Berkley/Jove Publishing Group,
200 Madison Avenue, New York, NY 10016

chapter 1

LEIGH CLENCHED HER teeth so hard that pain shot down her neck. She couldn't believe what she was hearing.

She sucked in a gulp of air to steady her wildly beating heart. "I have traveled thousands of miles to join your expedition," she said in a voice of barely repressed fury. "And all at *your* request! Now you're telling me I can't go. Correct?" She glared at the tall man before her and waited for his response, her fingernails stabbing into the palms of her hands.

Paulo Silva walked from behind his desk to stand in front of her. *"Miss Harris,* you are correct," he answered, his voice frosty as winter.

She straightened, her back rigid with anger. "Why? Or am I allowed to know the reason?"

Paulo inclined his head, a black curl falling onto his

forehead. Brushing it back and walking to a chair, he gestured for her to sit down.

She shook her head. "I'll remain standing."

He shrugged. "Suit yourself." He sat, then appraised her with piercing intensity.

Leigh returned his appraisal, her gaze traveling over the well-built Brazilian. His eyes were so intense she felt as if he could read her innermost thoughts. She dropped her gaze to his firm mouth, to the cleft in his chin. Very Latin, she thought, the black hair that curled on the nape of his neck, the finely sculptured nose, the bronze skin that denoted a man who liked the outdoors. A shiver worked its way through her.

Paulo spoke her name and her heart lurched. He flicked a piece of lint from his black silk shirt, his voice deep as he continued. "Of course, you know why you aren't going. Because, Dr. Harris, your letter led me to believe you were a man, not a woman." With a suggestive male look his gaze moved down the length of her. "And, I might add, a beautiful woman at that, which makes it even more important that I refuse you permission to go on my expedition." His fingers touched a copper medallion that was nestled in the black hair of his chest.

He sounded just like Frank! Her hands balled into fists at her sides. "Mr. Silva, I am an excellent botanist with a good recommendation from the university. I want to go with you to the Amazon. That region is a botanical paradise. I wish you'd reconsider."

"There will be six men on the expedition. I don't want any problems. And, believe me, if I allowed a woman to come along there would be problems. Go back to the United States, marry some man, and have a dozen children."

Bristling with anger, Leigh crossed the distance between them and towered over the seated Paulo. "I have no intention of causing any problems. I'm not interested in—in..." A slow wave of warmth moved up her neck to cover her cheeks as he studied her with amusement gleaming in his dark eyes.

"In taking a lover, Miss Harris?" He laughed, the sound making the color in her cheeks deepen.

"Yes, Mr. Silva," she said with all the pride she could muster.

"That's what you say now, but when we are deep in the Amazon what will you do to entertain yourself at night?"

Leigh opened her mouth then clamped it shut, rage blocking all rational thoughts from her mind except one: He's an arrogant bastard!

She stepped back, her eyes wide, and watched as he rose and strode to a liquor cabinet.

"Would you care for a drink before you go? You look as if you could use one."

"No thank you," she said tersely.

He dropped two ice cubes into a glass, then poured himself some whiskey. He faced her, and the silence between them grew until Leigh thought she would scream.

"I suggest you use this trip as a vacation," he said in a low, commanding voice. "I'll pay your expenses for two weeks to make up for the inconvenience of coming to Rio."

"How kind of you, Mr. Silva. I left a good job at the university to come to Brazil, and you tell me that I can have a two-week paid vacation, and all will be fine with the world." She waved her hand. "Well, no thanks."

Leigh whirled and strode across the study. At the door she turned. "I'm staying at the Rio Sheraton. I hope you'll think it over and decide differently. Your expedition leaves in three days. Do you want to postpone it to look for another botanist?" She yanked the door open.

"Dr. Harris."

She glanced back over her shoulder. "Yes?"

"It's grown dark outside since you came. Can you find your way back to the hotel? Let me . . ."

"I don't need your help. I have a good sense of direction and will have no trouble finding my way back. Good night, Mr. Silva." Leigh slammed the door behind her and walked across the spacious entrance hall to the front doors.

Outside she paused and let the warm perfumed breeze wash over her, hoping it would help calm her. She gazed upward at the glittering stars in the velvet, black sky, then drew in deep breaths and headed for her rented car.

Sliding behind the steering wheel, she took one last look at the white brick mansion with a veranda that ran the length of its front. After starting the engine and shifting into drive, she resisted the urge to press her foot on the accelerator and screech away from his house.

"I can't believe that man!" she said aloud and turned onto the street in front of his house, gripping the steering wheel tighter until her hands ached and her knuckles were white.

But, she admitted, she had signed the letter to him as L. H. Harris on purpose, making sure there was no reference to *Leigh* Harris in any of the papers she'd sent him. He had a right to be angry with her and an inner voice chided her that she had little justification for her own outrage.

She remembered the spring day she had learned about Paulo Silva's expedition and again felt the tingling sensation that thoughts of traveling to the Amazon and working there had inspired. This was a once-in-a-lifetime opportunity. And now she'd blown it!

No! He had no right to say those things to her. He was a stubborn, arrogant man who thought a woman belonged in the kitchen. Just like her ex-fiancé. Rage flamed into an all-consuming fire. Blood pounded in her ears, her eyes misted with tears of frustration and anger. She hadn't let Frank dictate her future and she wouldn't let Paulo Silva!

When Leigh turned onto another street, she could see Paulo's taunting face. She could hear his laughter. Blinking back the tears, she shook her head. Again the dark, lonely road stretched before her. With a sigh she slowed the car but could see no signs that were familiar, only a new suburban housing project with unfinished homes and deserted streets.

No streetlights! No street signs! She was lost!

Inching the car forward, Leigh noticed lights in the distance and pressed the accelerator. She halted the car at the end of the road, squinted, then sighed when she saw that the lights were still about a hundred feet distant from her.

This was where being proud and stubborn got her— lost.

"I can't stay here," she whispered and opened the car door, intending to seek help.

Cautiously, she walked across the clearing toward the lights. Her eyes darted from side to side, taking in the dark shadows that the plants and trees cast on the ground. Something moved on her left and she searched the darkness while quickening her pace. Within a few yards of the lights, she halted and a small gasp escaped her lips at the sight of four wooden posts with red and black ribbons covering them. The posts were joined by lengths of rope that enclosed the area where two women and a man stood.

She stepped into a patch of deep shadow and watched, wide-eyed, as the man put several shiny objects onto a circle that had been drawn in the earth. Her throat closed as she stared at a bowl filled with red liquid which he placed in the center of the circle.

The man took a single puff on the cigar in his mouth,

then poured a bottle of liquor on the ground. He waved his arms, his face contorted.

Leigh's stomach knotted. She had absolutely no business here. What would those three people do if they discovered her—an intruder, a foreigner as well—watching their strange ritual?

The man made a cross with two cigars and the younger of the women began to beat a drum as she chanted in a shrill voice.

Rooted to the spot, afraid to move and risk attracting their attention, Leigh stared at the scene before her while the man lit several candles and placed them around the bowl. He buried an envelope in front of the bowl, then blew smoke over the dirt, making Leigh shiver even more, for the air seemed to be charged with tension.

The man grabbed another bottle of liquor and downed the contents in a few gulps. Leigh clamped her teeth against her lower lip as the drum increased its beat. The man whirled and twisted to the sound, sweat drenching him, his white shirt clinging to him, his face contorting as he spat on the ground.

"Exú, come forth. Look, there are cigars and alcohol for you. Take these beautiful gifts and help me."

The man's assistant pounded the drum harder and harder, the sound bombarding Leigh. She wanted to clasp her hands over her ears, but she remained frozen.

She was dreaming. She shook her head. *It was all just a dream.*

The man spun around and Leigh knew he'd spotted her. He screamed and shook his fist. Leigh raced toward her car.

She heard the man continuing to rant and shout.

Only a few more yards, she thought. The sound of the drum seemed to force her to move more quickly. Then, at last, she was at the car. She yanked open the door and collapsed into her seat, taking in lungsful of air to steady her galloping heartbeat. Laying her head on the steering wheel, she closed her eyes. Confused thoughts crowded her mind. She sat up, turned the key, and started the car, then clenched the steering wheel and looked straight ahead.

As she guided the car away from the deserted area, her stomach tightened into a hard knot. The wildness of the ceremony she had witnessed rolled in a jumble through her mind.

Searching the stretch of dark road, she saw another street ahead and turned into it. Still, the hair on the back of her neck tingled, and she imagined eyes drilling into her. She inhaled, then exhaled slowly, and her heartbeat quieted. She spotted a main road ahead. Rational thought returned and she relaxed her grip on the steering wheel.

Bright lights of other cars were coming toward her, and she released a slow sigh. "I'm safe," she murmured, regretting her impulsive refusal of Paulo Silva's assistance. Rio was so different from the small college town she'd lived in most of her life. *So different*. Who—or what—was Exú?

chapter 2

A FAINT SOUND filtered through the sleep that clung to Leigh's mind, and she rolled over, placing the pillow over her head, but the ringing persisted. She flung the pillow away and fumbled for the phone.

"*Alô*, Leigh Harris," she whispered, her mind clouded with sleep.

"*Bom dia.*"

Leigh bolted up in bed, her mind snapping to alertness. Paulo Silva! She couldn't mistake that deep, rich voice with the slight accent.

"And to what do I owe this call, Mr. Silva?" Leigh glanced at the clock and noticed that it was seven in the morning. "Isn't it a little early for you to be calling to wish me a nice trip home?" Her voice was filled with sarcasm.

"If this is what I'll be greeted with every morning in the jungle, then I might reconsider my decision of last night to allow you to come on the expedition."

Leigh's breath caught in her throat, and she nearly dropped the receiver as a wave of excitement rippled through her.

"Are you serious?" she asked finally, her hand quivering as she held the phone to her ear.

"I don't joke, Dr. Harris. Frankly, you were right about finding another botanist. I don't have the time. I want to leave in two days and I need one now. You're the only one available at this time so I must accept you."

"Thanks."

"Let's get one thing straight. I don't want you on the expedition, but you're the only one I can take. If I could find another botanist—a man—I would take him. I don't want any trouble, *Miss Harris*. Do I make myself perfectly clear?"

"Too clear." Leigh bit her lower lip to stifle a retort, but the words tumbled from her mouth as her anger rose. "I have a mind not to accept your *kind* offer, Mr. Silva."

He laughed. "Refusal might cross your mind but you'll accept the offer. Am I not correct?"

Leigh squeezed her eyes shut and ground her teeth. I wish I didn't want to go so badly, she thought. Choking rage collected in her throat as the thumping beat of her heart hammered against her breasts.

"I accept," she said in a bare whisper.

"What did you say?"

Louder she said, "I accept, Mr. Silva."

"Good. Now be ready in an hour. I'm picking you up to take you on a boat ride in the bay."

Leigh stiffened. "I'm afraid I have other plans. Sleep, for one." The rage had a firm grip on her now.

"Oh, you didn't get enough sleep last night?"

"Good day, Mr. Silva."

Leigh started to slam down the receiver when she heard him say, "I want you to come this morning so you can meet one of the members of the expedition. I'll see you in one hour. I'll be in the hotel lobby."

Then Leigh heard the dial tone and felt liquid fire surge through her veins. The nerve of that man, she thought. So overbearing. She'd be damned if she'd . . .

She jerked the sheets back and slid her feet to the floor. "Don't kid yourself, Leigh. You're going," she said aloud and padded to the closet.

Selecting a pair of white cotton slacks and a navy-blue halter top, she laid them on the bed and walked into the bathroom. A quick inspection in the mirror revealed deep shadows under her eyes.

Her father's often-repeated description of her eyes came back to her. "Leigh, you have your mother's eyes. They're your best asset. They're so large that when I look into them I think of two emeralds fringed in black feathers."

Laughing, Leigh splashed cold water on her face. Right now those two emeralds didn't look good.

A frown descended over her features as she remembered the reason she had tossed and turned most of the night. That—ceremony? She supposed that's what it was . . . some kind of ceremony she'd witnessed.

A shudder streaked down her spine as she thought about the twisted, contorted face of the man as he danced to the beat of the drum. Why did she always plunge into a situation without thinking about the consequences? She should have let Paulo Silva take her home—pride or no pride—because she didn't know her way around Rio.

She shrugged. One day she'd *have* to learn not to let her Irish temper get the best of her.

Her thick auburn hair hung about her shoulders, the ends curling. Gathering her hair into a ponytail, she examined her face in the mirror. "To pale," she said aloud.

"Must get some sun before I leave for the Amazon." She let her hair drop into place as she noticed a few freckles on the tip of her small, straight nose and rubbed at them. "Not much you can do about those."

After cleaning her teeth, she walked into the outer room and began to dress. She ran a brush through her long hair, then placed a floppy hat on her head.

Paulo Silva was waiting for her by the bar in the lobby. A blush spread across her cheeks as his raking gaze swept down the length of her, appraising, assessing. When he looked her in the eye, a lazy hint of a smile touched his features.

Her eyes dropped to the glistening red medallion around his neck. The copper had the brilliance of the moon absorbing the sun's rays.

"That's a very unusual medallion," Leigh said when she stood in front of him.

A guarded look slipped over his features, reminding her of a cornered jungle cat.

"It was a gift," Paulo finally said. His voice held a wary note.

Suddenly the air surrounding Leigh felt cold, as if the temperature had plunged twenty degrees in seconds, and her heart skipped a beat as she looked away from the copper medallion.

"We'd better get going." Paulo broke through the icy barrier she had felt circle her and placed a hand on her arm.

Warm fingers seared her flesh like a branding iron and she yanked her arm from his grasp, again feeling the coldness encompass her. What's wrong with me? she wondered. She hugged her arms to her, and slowly the heat of the morning sun touched her.

A formal, distant look entered Paulo's eyes. "Follow me, Dr. Harris." He guided her through the glass doors to a silver Jaguar.

"I like a woman who's on time. That's a good sign," he said as he pulled the car out into the stream of traffic.

Relishing the feel of the cool breeze, Leigh placed her hat in her lap and let the warmth of the sun caress her skin. Her attention went first to the tall mountains that towered over the road, then was drawn to the shimmering blue water with diamondlike sparkles glittering off its surface. On the beach some people lay on the white sand, sunning themselves and relaxing, while others played beach games or flirted.

As Paulo inched the car forward in the traffic on the Avenida Atlantica, Leigh saw young, muscular men exercising on bars set in the sand as women in *tangas* watched them. She smiled at the brief Brazilian bikinis the women wore. Nothing left to the imagination, she thought, and smiled.

Turning, she studied the people along the black-and-white mosaic promenade as Paulo's car picked up speed and he wove in and out of the heavy traffic. She brushed veils of hair from her face and settled back in the seat.

In the distance Leigh saw the Sugar Loaf and turned to Paulo to ask over the honking of the cars, "Is the view from the Sugar Loaf as beautiful as they say?"

He glanced at her. "Yes, but my favorite place to see Rio is from Corcovado."

"The Christ figure?"

He nodded. "Of course, the tourists have taken over. I don't go there often, but it does give you a beautiful, breathtaking view of the city."

"Maybe I'll be able to see it when we get back from the Amazon. I'm really looking forward to searching for this fernlike plant that you described in your letter. To think of finding a new plant and naming it!"

"That I'll leave to you, Dr. Harris."

"Of course, I'll have to classify the plant first, but that will be fun."

"As a chemist, I'm only interested in its properties as a potential drug. The rest you can take care of." He pulled into a parking space at the harbor.

Again, Leigh looked up at the Sugar Loaf to the right of them and thought of its majestic lines. "The guardian of Guanabara Bay," she whispered to herself. It hovered over them as if watching their every move.

She thought about Rio's history. Sugar Loaf mountain had loomed over the shiploads of slaves that were carried to Brazil from Africa. It had been there during the flight of the royal Portuguese family when Napoleon overran Portugal and for the victory celebrations when Brazil gained independence from Portugal.

A hand nudged her, bringing her back to the present, and she turned to Paulo. She again felt his touch like fire licking at her flesh.

He'd stopped the car and was staring intently at her. "Shall we go?" he asked in his low, deep voice.

Leigh was stunned for a moment. How could she be so angry at him one moment that she could hardly speak, then want to melt at his nearness? Confused at the feelings he provoked in her, she shook off the conflicting emotions and let him lead her. They went down a pier toward a yacht that was painted white with blue trim. Leigh admired the graceful lines of the boat, a smile touching her lips. She stepped onto the sleek, beautiful yacht, bracing herself to become accustomed to the movement of the water.

Paulo gripped her elbow and led her along the deck. When she entered a salon, she suppressed a gasp. It was magnificent. Plush beige carpet covered the floor and there were navy-blue velvet chairs and sofas. Rich mahogany wood and brass fittings shone as if they had just been polished to that high sheen.

From behind her Leigh heard a husky voice. "Is this the botanist you told me about, Paulo?"

She spun around and stared into the handsome face of a tall, thin man who flashed her a boyish smile. She returned his smile and nodded. "I'm afraid I'm the guilty party."

He thrust his hand out for her to shake. "I'm Jorge Bardi. I'll be on the expedition, too." He looked at Paulo. "This won't be as boring as I thought, Paulo. Congratulations on your selection of such a delightful botanist." Jorge's brown eyes twinkled with unconcealed interest.

Paulo scowled. "Jorge, remember we're going to the Amazon for only one thing. To find that plant." Turning sharply, he left the salon.

"I wish Paulo would loosen up some. Ever since his wife and family died..." Jorge whispered as if to himself, shaking his head as he stared at Paulo's retreating figure.

"Died?" Leigh repeated, shocked.

"Yes. We lost Carmen and the others two years ago." Jorge seemed lost in his own thoughts for a moment before he glanced down at Leigh and took her elbow, flashing her a brilliant smile. "Come, let's watch Paulo take the yacht out of the harbor."

"Does he pilot the yacht?" she asked.

"Sometimes. He does have a crew, though." Jorge raked his fingers through his curly brown hair and moved closer to her.

As the yacht moved out of its berth, Leigh leaned against the railing and breathed deeply of the sea air. When the shoreline was far away, she felt salt spray on her face and stepped back from the railing. Jorge moved even closer to her. "Let's talk," Jorge murmured. "I can think of several interesting topics for a conversation."

"You can?" An eyebrow rose.

"Us, for one."

"You think that will be interesting?" Leigh asked, a movement behind Jorge catching her attention.

When she looked past Jorge, she saw a tall woman with short black hair approaching them, the woman's graceful strides like a ballerina's. The proud tilt of the head, the long slender legs, and the straight posture completed the picture. But as the woman fixed a smile on her face, Leigh sensed that her interest ran deeper than mere curiosity.

"Who's this, Jorge?" the woman asked in Portuguese.

"Marte Costa, this is Leigh Harris. She'll be joining us on the expedition," Jorge answered in English.

"Oh?" Marte raised an eyebrow in surprise and studied Leigh. "I didn't think Paulo would take a woman on the trip." Her blue eyes narrowed.

Leigh forced herself to smile and said in Portuguese, "He had no choice."

Marte's eyes widened, and a pout tugged at the corners of her mouth. "I wish I could go," she said as she turned to Jorge and ran her finger down his shirt front. "You're the only one who can ever talk any sense into Paulo."

Jorge laughed. "You go? You wouldn't survive one hour in the jungle. You hate the heat and the insects. What do you think the jungle is?"

"But Paulo would be there. You're going to be gone for months while I'm stuck in Rio."

"Having fun as usual, Marte. I doubt you'll be bored even if Paulo isn't here. You always seem to find something to do with your time."

The pout deepened. "Still, it will be boring with you all gone," she said and lifted her shoulders in a shrug. "But I suppose I'll find something to entertain myself with."

She strolled aft and lounged in a chair, stretching out her long, tanned legs to get the most exposure of the sun. Leigh looked at her own white pants, then at Marte's peach-colored shorts, and wished she had thought to wear shorts.

"I could never picture Marte in the jungle," Jorge whispered. "Now *you,* you are different." His breath fanned Leigh's neck as he brushed away a strand of her hair.

Whirling, Leigh faced him, taking a step back. He was too fast, she thought, but then so many Latin men were. Not like Frank, who took her for granted, always believing she would do what he wanted.

She cocked her head to one side and asked, "Different? How?"

"You're petite, but I think you're stronger than most women—especially ones like Marte." He arched a brow. "Am I not right, Leigh?"

She flexed her muscles in her upper arm. "I never thought my muscles showed. I've taken great precautions to see that they don't bulge. I guess I'd better stop working out at the gym every day."

Jorge roared with laughter. "Working out at the gym! Do you really?"

"Well, I was just kidding about every day, but I do go to the university gym and play racketball three times a week."

"What else do you do with your spare time, Leigh Harris?"

She grew taut when Paulo's deep voice interrupted the conversation. Glancing over her shoulder, she watched him move toward her, instinctively stepping closer to Jorge as if he could offer some protection from the raw primitiveness that seemed to be so much a part of Paulo.

"It comforts me to know I won't have to worry about rescuing you every few minutes in the Amazon." Paulo's mouth curved into a smile, but his eyes remained cold. Leigh thought of an Arctic night and shivered when she looked into those icy depths.

"I have a garden and I like to read a lot," she said.

"Nothing very exciting, but I enjoy the quiet life."

"Which, for the next few months, won't be the case," Paulo said and stepped around her.

She watched him walk toward Marte, his movements reminding her of an animal on the prowl for its next victim. Why did she feel that she was the next victim? He had made it very clear how he felt about women, especially those who wanted a career.

Paulo sat next to Marte, their heads bent together in whispered conversation. Marte's features lit with a smile, her blue eyes sparkling as they roamed over Paulo.

"You know I'm really surprised that Paulo's letting you go on the expedition."

Leigh turned to face Jorge. "Why? I'm qualified."

"Because he thinks women belong at home raising children."

"Yes, he's already informed me of what I should be doing. Did he and his wife have any children?" Leigh asked, her question sounding breathless to her ears. Again she sought Paulo, his hard features softened in a smile as he talked with Marte.

Jorge pulled Leigh along the deck until they stood at the front of the yacht. "No. They were married ten years, but were having too much fun to have a family. I suppose, though, they would have soon because Paulo wanted children—an heir to inherit his pharmaceutical business."

Leigh gazed out across the blue stretch of water at the mountains in the background, the vivid colors of Rio scattered among the lush greenery of the landscape.

"I can't imagine Paulo having fun with anyone. He was so formal, so cold with me when I was at his house last night."

Jorge leaned on the railing next to her. "He used to be different. Such a playboy."

The atmosphere was charged as if a bolt of lightning

had struck the deck. Leigh searched Jorge's face, feeling as if their conversation was covering forbidden ground, as if Paulo would descend on them, his features twisted with anger.

Jorge met her gaze with sadness in his eyes. "She was very beautiful, Leigh."

"You and she must have been good friends. I'm sorry."

"We were friends—but then everyone loved her. If only . . ." With a toss of his head, Jorge indicated an area where they could sit and sun themselves. "Come, let's change the subject. I didn't mean to talk about something so depressing. I mean to pursue a beautiful woman and convince her to have dinner with me tonight." He took Leigh's hand and led her forward.

When she had stretched out on the deck chair, she said, "That would be nice. After last night I don't know if I want to leave my hotel after dark alone. Do you know who Exú is?"

Jorge's brown eyes widened. "Exú! Where in the world did you hear that name?"

"I got lost driving home from Mr. Silva's house and came upon some kind of ceremony. A man dancing to the beat of a drum, burying objects in the ground—it was spooky." Leigh hugged herself.

"Oh, Leigh, I bet! Do you know you were witnessing a Quimbanda ceremony?"

"Quimbanda? What's that?"

"Black magic, I guess you could say. The man was asking Exú to help him with an evil deed. People go to the priests of Quimbanda to have them work evil deeds for them—casting spells, causing illnesses—even death. I'm sorry to say it's practiced extensively in Brazil."

Leigh's throat tightened. "I thought black magic existed only in the movies—that it died out long ago. Do people really believe in that kind of thing today?"

Jorge took Leigh's hands within his, his features set in a serious expression. "Yes, Leigh. It's very strong in Brazil, but most Brazilians don't like to talk about it. There's a good side to Exú, though. Quimbanda exists, but most Brazilians believe and attend the ceremonies of Macumba—white magic."

"So this is where you two have gone. The cook has prepared lunch. Are you hungry?"

Leigh tensed, then turned and rose. Paulo stood a few feet from them, looking very handsome as he lounged against the railing with a smile brightening his features. All her senses reacted to the aura of power that surrounded him. As she walked past him, the air between them electrified.

"We are docking at Paquetá Island in a little while." Paulo stepped next to her as she walked toward the salon. "We can rent bicycles and ride around the island. Would you care to come?"

"You're asking for my opinion? I thought your style was to give orders." She shrank back when she saw a look of thunder spread across his sardonic features.

"Careful, Dr. Harris. No matter how much I want to leave in two days, I might postpone my expedition to replace a botanist." He brushed past her into the salon.

Her breathing became shallow. If she could put that man in his place just once, she thought, having him as a boss would be bearable.

"Don't let him bother you, Leigh," Jorge said, placing a hand on her elbow and opening the door for her.

"It's very hard to ignore him. But at least I have you to talk to. Thanks for making me feel at home."

Jorge bowed. "My pleasure."

When Leigh entered the salon, she saw a table laden with strange-looking food and Paulo gesturing toward it, his voice formal as he said, "In your honor, my chef has prepared dishes that are favorites of Brazilians." He moved to the table and spooned into a bowl a thick soup over a bed of rice. "This is *feijoada*." The dish was garnished with a bright green boiled leaf and three slices of orange.

When Paulo started to serve her a stuffed eggplant fried in cracker crumbs, she said, "I think the *feijoada* will be enough. One new thing at a time."

Taking the bowl, Leigh sat on a couch along the wall and took a glass of pale yellow liquid from Jorge. "I'm afraid to ask. This isn't lemonade?"

"It's a *batida* and should be drunk before you eat your *feijoada*."

Leigh looked at the glass, then wrinkled her nose. "What's in it? Or should I know?"

Grinning, Jorge answered, "Oh, nothing much. Just lemon juice and *cachaca*, a liquor made from sugarcane. It's safe to drink. Go ahead."

Leigh sipped the liquid and smiled. "That's not bad."

"Finish it before you eat." Jorge sat next to her on the couch.

"Why?"

"Because a *batida* makes the *feijoada* settle easier on the stomach. After eating the *feijoada* you have no energy. It's quite a filling dish."

"I'm not so sure I should eat it, then. Mr. Silva told me we would be bicycling around the island when we land."

"If you want, we can just walk along the beach. Paquetá Island is one of the most peaceful places near Rio. Cars and trucks aren't allowed. The only way you can travel on the island is walking or bicycling. I think you'll like this place. It's the quiet life, as you say."

After eating the *feijoada*, Leigh leaned back on the couch and closed her eyes. The peaceful calm of the yacht began to lull her to sleep, but as she felt herself drift toward sleep, a hand touched her arm.

"Leigh, we have landed at the island. Do you care to see it?"

Leigh's eyes fluttered open and she stared into Paulo's black ones, a strange gleam sparking his eyes.

He turned away and said, "You don't have to come. If you choose to nap, then do so." His voice was no longer gentle but curt.

"You're giving me a choice again? How kind."

Now why did I say that? she wondered, and gritted her teeth as a frown settled on Paulo's features.

Paulo pulled her to a standing position and thrust his face within inches of hers. She could smell his cologne and the faint scent of Marte's perfume. Leigh tried to pull free, but his grip tightened until she cried out.

"*Dr. Harris*, I have no control over what you do now, but when we leave in two days, I will. Remember that." His gaze bore into her. "Do you still want to go on the expedition? My word is *law* when we leave Rio."

Words dried in her throat, but Leigh nodded.

"Good. Then I'll leave you in Jorge's care. I'm staying on the island, so I won't see you until the party tomorrow night. It begins at six."

"Party?"

"Yes. A small celebration before the expedition departs the next day. I hope you're an early riser. We'll leave Rio at six in the morning. My driver will pick you up at five and take you to the airport."

Paulo turned abruptly and, without a backward glance, left the salon. Leigh clasped her hands to stop their shaking, but the fragrance of his cologne lingered in the air, making her intensely aware of his raw virility. As an icy shroud cloaked her, she balled her hands at her sides.

Leave Rio before it's too late! The warning flashed in her thoughts. Paulo Silva is a man who could hurt you! Sinking onto the couch, Leigh thought about her disastrous engagement to Frank and the promise she'd made to herself to control her own destiny. She felt strange then—as if Paulo Silva were her destiny. Stop it, she commanded herself. She wasn't the naive girl who'd fallen in love with her professor. No! Frank had taught her a great deal . . . a very great deal.

chapter 3

"JORGE, THIS IS unbelievable! I've never seen such a beautiful sight."

Leigh gazed down upon Rio, which looked like a jewel nestled in a bed of green velvet, her eyes traveling over the diamond white sea, glittering from the brilliant rays of the sun. Sucking in her breath, she held it for a long moment.

She pointed and turned to Jorge. "You can see the lagoon and the Jockey Club from here. And the Sugar Loaf! It looks so small. Not nearly as impressive as when we were standing beside it."

"I will not have you slight the Sugar Loaf," Jorge replied. "The view from it is breathtaking, but the Corcovado does stand high above Rio. It's comforting at night to look up into the mountains and see the figure of Christ with his outstretched arms guarding Rio." He placed an arm about her waist.

Leigh turned away from him and inspected the huge granite Christ statue. She craned her neck to get a glimpse of the face of the figure with its impassive expression, then stared at the Corcovado in awe until Jorge nudged her.

"Leigh, we'd better leave if we're going to make the party on time. Paulo expects us at six."

"And I suppose we shouldn't be late." Leigh glanced once more at the Christ figure, then at the city of Rio, sprawled among the coastal mountains for miles in every direction. Turning, she followed Jorge to his car.

As they descended from the mountains, Leigh watched the passing scenery. Everything was so green. Not like home, she thought, where it was fall and the trees were turning colors. It would be a long time, though, before she saw Kentucky again.

She sighed and focused her attention on the narrow winding road Jorge was navigating. The scenery faded from whitewashed houses of the well-to-do into the hillside shacks of the *favela*.

Jorge pointed toward the squatters' town and said, "The government is trying to do away with the *favela* but it will take time to move all these people into government-built housing."

"Rio is such a city of contrast. There are brightly painted houses of years ago next to modern skyscrapers. Such wealth and such poverty."

"I have traveled to many countries, but have never found a more beautiful city in the world. Rio outshines all others. I always return to my birthplace."

As the car climbed the side of another hill, the image of Paulo intruded into Leigh's thoughts for a brief moment, but she quickly banished it from her mind.

But when the car stopped in front of Paulo's mansion,

she felt a moment of apprehension. She knew she had been sheltered most of her life. For the first time she was really on her own, about to embark on an adventure she'd dreamed about ever since she had taken her first course in botany six years before. She felt a stab of alarm. She could handle the job, but could she handle Paulo Silva?

"Well, Dr. Harris and Jorge, it's good to see you." Paulo stepped into the entrance hall and closed his hand around hers to shake it. The gesture was both warm and suggestive.

Leigh felt the heat of his flesh against hers. But I'm so cold, she thought.

His dark, compelling gaze assessed her, a blush rising in her cheeks. She sucked in a deep breath. Was she misreading him? Could there really be such a smoldering look of desire hidden in the black depths of his eyes? She dropped her gaze and tugged her hand from his, mumbling, "Thank you."

She felt like a butterfly under a microscope and confusion pushed all thoughts from her mind but one—*she had to escape his piercing, probing eyes.*

She turned abruptly and moved swiftly away. Jorge caught up with Leigh, his laughter sounding too loud in the quiet of the house. Leigh halted and surveyed the area around her, her brows furrowed.

"Where does that corridor go?" she asked.

"He really does upset you, doesn't he?" But Jorge didn't demand an answer. "His laboratory is down there," he said gesturing toward a darkened hallway.

"He works at home? I thought he just ran his pharmaceutical company."

Jorge took her elbow and steered her toward the living room. "Paulo is a chemist first, a businessman second. That's why he's going on the expedition. Finding that plant of his is very important to him—almost an obsession."

The living room was brightly lit. Leigh's eyes roved over the thick, white carpet, deep blue sofas, a grand piano, and vases of cut flowers that filled the air with a sweet fragrance. Her gaze halted at a Renoir, then a Degas. She was sure they were originals, and that Paulo Silva was wealthy—very wealthy.

Suddenly she realized there were more people in this lovely room. Some were staring at her and Jorge. As Paulo stepped away from a group and moved toward them, she admired the cut of his dark gray silk suit which seemed to accent his muscular body. Again she was drawn to the medallion that hung in the V of his black silk shirt, open down the front. She realized he must wear it all the time, and felt mesmerized by that circle glittering in the lights.

"I'm sorry, Dr. Harris. I seem to have upset you. I didn't mean to," Paulo said, a hint of amusement in his voice.

She narrowed her eyes. "I'm sure you didn't, Mr. Silva."

"Paulo, please. We'll be working quite closely for the next several months. I think it's time you called me by my first name, *Leigh*."

As he spoke her name, caressing it, her heartbeat quickened. The sound on his tongue sent shivers down her spine.

What was wrong with her, she wondered as Paulo turned to Jorge and asked him about the preparations for the flight to the Amazon. She didn't want to become involved with any man, especially someone like Paulo Silva. He had too much self-assurance, too much pride. Too much...

"Let me introduce you to the rest of the crew, Leigh," he said and touched her arm.

She focused on his features as he spoke, watching his sensuous mouth move with his words. His intense black eyes gleamed as her gaze locked with his. She felt as if she were drowning in whirlpools of blackness.

Pulling her attention away, she scanned the room and caught sight of Marte, a drink in one hand, a cigarette in the other. The woman's blue eyes glinted with hatred, making Leigh step back from the force of her stare.

Paulo grasped Leigh's hand and pulled her toward a short blond man. "Leigh Harris, I want you to meet Carlos de Sousa. He'll be our guide."

She inclined her head, then found herself in front of a pair of men, each dark and tall.

"Miguel and João de Andrade are also accompanying us as my assistants."

"I thought Jorge was your assistant," Leigh said.

Tossing back his head, Paulo laughed. "Hardly. Jorge is a friend who has persuaded me to take him along on this adventure. Now, what can I fix you to drink?"

"Since coming to Rio I've tasted the most delicious fruit drinks. Whatever you have along that line will be fine. Since I must wake up before the crack of dawn tomorrow, I want to be sharp." She leveled him a penetrating look. "I wouldn't want to oversleep. I've a feeling my boss would leave me behind."

A twinkle gleamed in the depths of his eyes. "But I hear your employer is kind and considerate. I can't imagine him doing something like that. But he probably would storm up to your room and bang on your door until you awoke, then drag you downstairs to his car."

"That doesn't sound kind and considerate to me. In fact, it's more like the picture I've formed of him."

The corners of his mouth turned up slightly as Paulo tried to contain a smile. He stepped closer and whispered near her ear, "Then I must try to change your opinion of him." He turned and walked to the bar where he ordered a scotch on the rocks for himself and a drink of freshly squeezed fruit juice for her.

Leigh watched him stroll toward her with a drink in each hand, his fluid movements reminding her of a cat stalking its prey, graceful and determined. Somehow she knew that she had to be very careful if she wasn't going to fall victim to him.

Looking away, she saw Marte talking with Carlos, her face filled with anger. As Marte directed a look at her, Leigh turned away, a frown capturing her features, and stared at the French doors, noticing that it was beginning to grow dark outside.

"I was gone for only a few minutes. Why the frown, Leigh?" Paulo handed her a frosted glass.

Warmth encased her when she heard him say her name, and she looked up into his eyes with a smile on her face. "You certainly have a high opinion of your companionship."

He bowed. "Why, of course. If I didn't, who would? Come, I want to show you my garden before it gets too dark. It's my pride. You said one of your hobbies was gardening, so you might appreciate my efforts."

When Leigh saw the garden from the top step of the terrace, her eyes grew round in delight at its beauty. A rainbow of colors stretched before her. Row upon row of bright yellows, deep reds, royal purples, sky blues spread across the lawn below her.

"The fountain!" she exclaimed, her attention drawn toward the center of the garden. Her gaze followed a row of palm trees that led to a waterfall. The water tumbled down into a basin where it sprayed up in a circle to fall again in droplets. She watched the lighted water change from pink to green then to a deep gold.

She turned to Paulo. "It's beautiful! Do you work in the garden yourself?" The cool evening breeze caressed her body, and she pulled her shawl tighter about her shoulders.

"When I have time, which lately hasn't been very often." He walked down the stairs to the stone path that wound between the rows of flowers and pointed to the right. "Below that terrace I built a swimming pool. Let me show you."

She followed him through the rose section until they reached steps that led to the lower area of the garden. She gasped. Before her lay a pool. No, a tropical lake, she decided. Another waterfall replenished the pool, and brown stones covered the bottom and sides, making it resemble a lagoon on a tropical island. Where's the native that dives off the ledge? she wondered and smiled at the thought.

"You must spend a lot of time here," she said. "It's so peaceful. I don't think I'd ever leave." The water held the deep rosy hue of the sunset, and when she looked up at Paulo, he smiled down at her. For a long moment she stared into his dark eyes. The only sounds were the song of a bird in a nearby tree and the splash of the waterfall. Time seemed to stand still as he leaned closer to her and bent his head toward her mouth.

Her heartbeat stopped for a brief second as she waited for their lips to touch. Suddenly wanting him to kiss her, she closed her eyes and reached toward him. But when she sensed him move away, she opened her eyes, her stomach muscles constricting. As he turned away from her, she brought her hand up and touched her cheek, feeling the warmth of her cheek beneath her fingertips.

"I think you should return to the party," he said in a throaty voice, a steeliness in his words.

Humiliated, Leigh stared at his rigid back for what seemed like an eternity before she spun on her heel and fled from the garden. She raced up the steps to the terrace and collided with Jorge, who steadied her and examined her features.

"What happened? Did the boss man bite?" he asked, laughter lacing his voice.

"I don't understand that man. One minute he's friendly, the next he's angry, and I don't know why."

Jorge cradled her to him and moved away from the light that streamed from the French doors. "Don't let him bother you—ever since the fire two years ago, he's been very moody."

"Fire?"

"That's how his wife, father, and sister were killed."

A numbness set in. "I didn't know," she whispered.

Jorge squeezed her hand. "Let me get you a drink."

As Leigh watched Jorge walk away, the numbness took a firm hold, mingling with her confusion and hurt. She had wanted Paulo to kiss her, she thought. But it wouldn't work between them. They were like oil and water, from two different worlds.

"If it isn't Miss Harris. Good evening. Did you have a nice walk in the garden *with Paulo?*"

Leigh winced at the bitterness in Marte's voice. She straightened to her full height and tilted her chin. "I don't believe it's any of your business, Miss Costa. Now, if you'll excuse me . . ."

"Just a minute. It *is* my business. Paulo's going to marry me one day. I don't like the idea of you going on this expedition with him."

"Then I suggest you talk with Paulo." Leigh stormed into the house, anger trembling through her as goose bumps rose on the nape of her neck.

She halted in the entrance hall and listened a moment to the chattering voices coming from the living room. She needed someplace quiet to think. Stepping away from the living room, she opened a door across from it.

When she entered the room, her attention became riveted on a picture hanging over the mantel. The woman was beautiful. But who was she? Her violet eyes captured Leigh's in a trance. It must be Carmen, Leigh decided, and rubbed her arms as a chill spread over her, a feeling of despondency following.

chapter 4

LEIGH WALKED THROUGH her dark hotel room and out onto the balcony. The world was bathed in bright moonlight and the air was humid. Despite the heat, a shiver ran up her spine when she remembered the portrait of Carmen, whose painted face had seemed to laugh at her, to tell her that Paulo was hers *forever*.

Leigh let the peaceful night soothe her. Hundreds of stars sparkled in the clear sky. Waves below her crashed against the beach and sounds of the band playing a samba drifted to her on a breeze. With a sigh, she started to turn when her attention was caught by the Corcovado on top of its mountain. Her breath caught as she stared at the Christ figure, the base of the statue shrouded in a heavy mist. Golden lights lit up the figure in the blackness that surrounded it. She gazed at the Christ figure for long moments and fingered the silk of her gown.

It would be a long time before she wore something like this again. The plain cotton slacks and shirt that would become her outfit tomorrow were practical but hardly glamorous.

Leigh undressed in the dark and slipped between the cool sheets. She glanced once more at the Corcovado before rolling onto her side. Violet eyes filled the black void as she closed her own eyes. She pulled the sheet up around her neck, her eyes snapping open. "Don't think about Carmen," she told herself fiercely. She had a job to do and couldn't let anything interfere. Paulo Silva was just a man—her boss, and nothing more!

Leigh felt the vibrations of the engines as the plane taxied to the end of the runway. She dug her fingernails into the padded arms of the chair and squeezed her eyes shut.

"Are you scared, Leigh?" Jorge asked.

With her eyes still closed, she nodded. She felt herself being pulled back into the softness of the chair as the wheels retracted into the belly of the plane. She opened her eyes and stared straight ahead. A hand closed over hers, and she turned with a half-smile.

"Do you fly much?" Jorge asked, his mouth drawn in a tight line, apparently to keep from laughing.

"The answer is no. Go ahead and laugh. You're dying to. I'm perfectly fine except on takeoffs and landings."

His eyes twinkled. "Oh, I see. Well, we have a couple of hours to prepare you for the landing."

"Don't be so smug," Leigh retorted. "I'm sure you have your own secret fears."

He shook his head. "Why should I? If it's my time to go, then nothing *I* can do will stop it." He shrugged.

"So, you don't think you control your own destiny? Well, Mr. Bardi, I *do* have something to say about my life." She twisted her head around to look out the window. The ocean was below, but to the left, the faint line of the coast could be seen. She watched as the waves broke over the sand, one after another, until the pilot headed the plane inland and she could no longer see the ocean, only green and brown.

She heard Jorge unsnap his seat belt and leave, then stared a moment longer out the window before fumbling in her tote bag for a book. She read the first sentence three times and closed it. It was no use; she couldn't concentrate. She tingled with anticipation. Two more hours and she'd be there. The Amazon! Finally!

"From the look on your face, it must be a happy thought," Paulo said next to her.

Leigh tensed as she looked at his mouth and thought of the night before. What would it be like to be kissed by him? She remembered his coldness toward her, coldness like dry ice that could burn her, burn her badly.

Aloud Leigh finally said, "I was smiling because I was thinking about the Amazon. I've dreamed of going there for years."

Paulo's features became serious. "Leigh, the Amazon is hard on a man, let alone a woman. I still have reservations about taking you. So many people have been lost in the jungle or killed. Almost everyone's health is affected by the heat and insects. You know that."

She turned to face him. "Yes! But it's probably one of the last places on earth where there are unknown plants. That's why both of us are going. Do you really believe in this plant that has miraculous properties for healing wounds and burns?"

"I have proof. I've seen the results of what it can do. A man I know was burned over thirty percent of his body and the Indians of the area where we're going spread a paste over his burns every day for five days. He was healed from second-degree burns in that short time with a minimum of pain and no infection. Within a month his scars had disappeared completely. It was unbelievable!"

"A miracle, if it's true. I'd spend the amount of money you are spending to find out, too, if I could."

"I think this fern will have other benefits as well. It seems to heal the skin rapidly, so the possibilities for closing wounds, treating skin cancer, and fighting infections are enormous. . . ."

Leigh heard the excitement in his voice and sensed a driving determination in him that was almost an obsession. Was it, she wondered, because his wife and family died in a fire?

". . . of course, the problem is where the Indian tribe is located," he was saying. "This tribe was completely isolated from civilization until recently and since then only my friend in the Indian Department has been there. He's the one who told me about the paste. I trust him. Soon the tribe will be exposed to the outside world and I want the plant before that happens."

"But if they live so far in the jungle, it will take years for that to happen." Leigh wanted to reach out and smooth the lines of worry from his brow.

"The exposure will take place more slowly than with some tribes because of where they live, but it will happen." Paulo clenched his hands. "The Amazon is opening up to the outside world more and more every day and, before long, every part of the jungle will have been explored. We need the raw resources the land has to offer."

"You're lucky this friend came to you."

Paulo stared past Leigh. "He's my brother-in-law. He'll be at the mission waiting for us. He's the only person who knows exactly where the tribe is located." His mouth thinned into a tight smile, and he seemed lost in his own thoughts. Then almost to himself he whispered, "I haven't seen him in over a year. Carmen and he were twins."

Twins! Again Leigh felt those violet eyes staring down at her. She clasped her hands tightly in her lap.

Paulo stood up. "We'll be landing soon," he said in a clipped voice, then turned and walked toward the cockpit.

Leigh watched him disappear, closing the door behind him. Would Paulo's brother-in-law look like his twin sister, with those same violet eyes? She shivered at the thought.

As the plane descended and the wheels locked into place, Leigh stiffened, closing her eyes. "I see you're ready to land, Leigh," Jorge said, slipping into the seat next to her.

She gripped the arms of the seat and waited, holding her breath until the plane landed with a light bump and slowed to a complete stop. Outside the jungle was only a few yards from her window. She unbuckled her seat belt and rose, her legs wobbly, then leaned across the opposite seats and watched two men approach the airplane. One wore the black robes of a priest and the other white slacks and a white shirt. Her gaze lingered on the man in white, who smiled as the plane door opened, then moved forward to shake Paulo's hand as he leaped to the ground.

The man's black hair was ruffled by the breeze, his skin a golden tan. He stood with his feet planted slightly apart, and he had broad shoulders and muscular legs outlined by tightly fitted pants. His face looked like a masculine version of Carmen.

When Leigh emerged moments later, he extended his hand. Despite the friendly gesture, there was a hard glint in the depths of his purple eyes that made her flinch. She shrank back against Paulo, whose hands closed around her arms.

Near her ear Paulo said, "This is Marcus Menezes. Marcus, Leigh Harris, our botanist for the expedition."

"The expedition!" Marcus exploded. "But she's a

woman! We don't need trouble like that on this trip. We're traveling into dense jungle." He shot Paulo a penetrating look that would have made most men wary. "Or had you forgotten that, *friend?*"

Paulo stepped around Leigh and clasped his brother-in-law on the shoulder, pulling him away. "No, I haven't. She's in excellent shape. I didn't have any choice in the matter. I'll explain later." He walked swiftly toward a cluster of small buildings. "Over a cool drink, I'll explain. This heat is ten times worse than in Rio."

"That's just the point..."

Leigh strained to hear the rest of what Marcus was saying, but his voice faded as the two men walked away. Did they all think a woman should only live to get married and have children? That a career couldn't be important to a woman? Were all men like Frank?

"Leigh, this is Father Jose," Jorge said, interrupting her thoughts. "He runs a mission for the church."

As Leigh turned, the priest smiled and said, "I'm sure after the long plane ride you'll want to rest. Around here we spend the middle part of the day napping. You'll find it helps to cope with the heat."

Leigh smiled back at him. "I certainly understand what you mean. Where will I be staying?"

Father Jose extended his arm. "Come this way and I'll be glad to show you to your quarters for the night." As they walked toward the buildings, he continued. "It's a shame you won't be staying for several days. I rarely have visitors and sometimes I miss the outside world."

"Are you the only person working here?"

He shook his head. "There is my assistant, Father Pedro, and Dr. Melo. Other than the three of us, there are only Indians who drift into the mission for help. We have a small hospital, a church, and I run a school for the children of the area."

Leigh climbed the steps to a porch circling a white

wooden house and went inside, where the coolness of
the interior enveloped her. Paulo and Marcus stood in
front of her, Marcus's features set in a scowl.

Paulo nodded to Father Jose and said, "Thank you
again for allowing us to stay here for the night. This
mission is the nearest to the area we are traveling to."

The priest inclined his head. "It's my pleasure. Now,
Miss Harris, your room is this way." He walked a few
steps to a door and thrust it open.

Leigh entered the small bedroom and quickly noted
the sparse furniture, old, but neat. Placing her tote bag
on the chest, she turned to the priest. "Thank you, Father
Jose. This is nice."

"If I can do anything for you, please let me know."
He smiled. "The noonday meal will be served in an
hour."

After Father Jose closed the door behind him, she sat
on the bed and kicked off her shoes, then lay back, her
head on the pillow. She stared at the single bulb that
dangled from the ceiling on a short wire. Her eyelids
grew heavy as the heat overpowered her, and she slipped
toward the cool blackness of sleep.

After dinner later that day, Leigh stood on the porch
and leaned against a post. Every moment was an effort
in the stifling heat. Toward the west she saw the vivid
orange of the sun mingle with the blue of the sky. The
scent of damp foliage hung heavy in the air. She scanned
the line of trees that made a natural barrier around the
compound and watched a flock of brightly colored birds
take flight and disappear in the direction of the river she
glimpsed through the dense vegetation. After listening
to the chorus of insects for a moment longer she turned
to go inside but stopped, following the movements of a
man as he emerged from the shadows.

"Good day, Leigh," Paulo greeted her as he ran his

hand across the back of his neck. "It's certainly a lot cooler than earlier today. At times the heat becomes unbearable in the jungle. I hope you realize all that's in store for you."

"I can take care of myself. I'm just as capable of withstanding the heat as you are," she assured him.

"Oh?" He arched a brow, mockery dancing in his eyes.

"I suppose you think men can withstand heat better than women," she commented. "Certainly Mr. Menezes does. Do you two know something I don't, Mr. Silva?"

"As a matter of fact, *Miss Harris,* I *do* think men are better able to handle most everything."

Leigh straightened. "Oh—*most* everything," she repeated, venom dripping from her voice.

As Paulo stepped closer, Leigh backed away, then turned and hurried toward the river. Once well away from the house, she slowed her pace. At the water's edge, she sat and stared at the brownish water rushing over stones and boulders, the minutes fusing into an hour.

Suddenly she realized that it had grown dark, dusk quickly fading into the blackness of night. Damn it, she knew better than to be caught in the jungle after dark— especially without a flashlight. Why did she always let Paulo get to her?

She started toward the mission, squinting her eyes and searching the path ahead of her as the darkness settled around her. A laugh formed in her throat but didn't reach her lips as she recalled how she'd assured Paulo she could take care of herself!

An animal's cry invaded the darkness and she froze. Seconds later she whirled toward the sound of rustling underbrush and felt a cold sweat engulf her body as she imagined a snarling jaguar leaping toward her. She batted at the tears the illusion provoked and tried to move her legs, but they felt like lead weights.

"Run, run!" her mind dictated, but her legs would not respond to the command.

Something brushed her arm and she gasped in sudden terror. Fingers closed about her upper arm to spin her around, and she felt a scream climb into her throat.

"What are you doing out here alone in the dark? Don't you know the dangers of the jungle at night?" Paulo's voice lashed out at her. "I was right! Women have no place in the Amazon."

Her confusion vanished as she felt the force of his words. She couldn't see his features, but she knew what he would look like with his mouth drawn in a thin line, his black eyes narrowed with a hard gleam in their depths, and his brow lined with anger.

"I didn't realize the sun sets so rapidly here," she said inwardly grimacing at the hollow-sounding excuse.

His fingers dug into her flesh. "I think we'll have to have a talk about the dangers of the jungle before we leave. You don't seem to know what you're getting into."

He pulled her along the path, but Leigh jerked her arm from his iron grip. "I know all about the Amazon. I've read every book about the jungle I could get my hands on."

Paulo pivoted. "Then why were you at the river after dark?"

"I was . . ."

"What? Angry at me?"

"Angry at you! Why should I be? All you've told me is how I should be clothed in an apron, holding a baby in one arm and stirring the dinner on the stove with the other."

Before she knew it, his arms had encircled her. He was pulling her closer to him. His kiss was fierce at first, bruising her lips into submission; it then became gentle as it deepened into a possession. Her mind whirled with new sensations and a flame of desire ignited deep within her. Every sense she possessed swirled from his forcefulness. She melted against his lean, hard frame and returned his kisses with an ardor that surprised her.

Suddenly he pushed her away and commanded in a harsh voice that cut the air with its sharpness, "Follow me!"

For a brief moment Leigh thought her legs wouldn't function as she watched Paulo stalk away from her. She ran her fingers across her bruised lips and felt the tingling sensation die when her cold fingertips brushed her mouth.

"Are you going to stand there all night?" he shouted back at her.

Her brows knitted, she began to follow him as he returned to the mission. How would she survive two months in the jungle with *him?*

She felt overpowered by the disturbing intensity that charged the air like an electrical storm. Halting at the edge of the compound, she watched Paulo walk toward the calm, civilized light of the hospital. With a sigh she resumed her steps, marveling at the contrast between this brooding, unpredictable man who tormented her, and the peaceful mission.

chapter 5

THOUGH SHE TRIED to force her food past the tightness in her throat, Leigh still shook from the intense emotions that Paulo had evoked in her at the river. She couldn't forget the demanding kiss that had sought to possess her or his anger, a reaction that troubled her more than she wanted to admit.

Why had he kissed her with such passion one minute only to turn away in anger the next? Was he attempting to exert his mastery over her, to show her he could arouse her but not be affected himself? Or, she thought suddenly, was he affected and trying to keep his distance because of the expedition? Before she could sort out these questions, Father Jose spoke, bringing her back to the present.

"I gather you will all be leaving at dawn tomorrow

morning," he said in an attempt to start a conversation at the table.

"It will take at least a week to travel to the Indian village. I want to travel as much as we can each day." Paulo's voice sounded tight with impatience.

"Yes, I can understand your desire not to stay in the jungle any longer than you need to, but don't push yourselves too hard. Remember the jungle is a cruel place," warned Father Jose.

That seemed to be all Leigh had heard in the last few days. As Paulo's penetrating gaze fell on her, she became even more aware of the dangers that the jungle could pose for someone—be they male or female. But worse than that she was acutely conscious of the dangers of being so close to Paulo for such a long time.

"We should do just fine, providing everyone carries his own load," Marcus commented, directing his attention toward Leigh.

Her spine stiffened as she met his accusing look. "I'm sure everyone will. Are you having doubts about going on this expedition, Mr. Menezes?"

His violet eyes turned a deep purple as they bored into her. "No, I have no doubts about *my* ability in the jungle. I've lived in this climate for months. But not everyone on the expedition knows what he or *she* is getting into."

An innocent look stole over her features. "Oh, but I thought everyone had been briefed by Paulo."

Marcus smiled but his eyes remained cold. "Apparently not everyone, Miss Harris."

Inside, Leigh seethed, but only her clenched hands revealed her anger. First Paulo and now Marcus. Did all Latin men think women were only good to raise babies and to run a house? She thought of the long journey ahead with days of trudging through jungle, but what bothered her the most was knowing she would have to be constantly proving herself to Marcus—and Paulo. *Especially Paulo.* And prove herself she would. She was determined to make it on her own without their help. They would take back their words by the end of this trip she swore to herself.

Directing a question at her, Father Jose pulled Leigh's attention away from her raging emotions. "Dr. Harris, I'd hoped to be able to show you the hospital, but I can see it's too late if you all are going to start out so early tomorrow. Perhaps when you return you'd like to see it?"

"I'd like that, Father Jose." Rising, Leigh continued, "But you're right. If I want to be ready at dawn, I'd better be thinking of bed. Excuse me, gentlemen."

All she really wanted was to escape the piercing appraisal that Paulo leveled at her. She remembered his earlier threat of discussing "the perils of the Amazon" with her, a discussion she didn't relish at all. She laughed silently, thinking that "discussion" wasn't the correct word to use. More like a lecture, she thought.

Sitting on her bed in the quiet of her room, she listened to the chorus of insects which was occasionally broken by the shriek of a monkey or the raucous call of a macaw. Again Paulo's kiss intruded into her thoughts, making sleep impossible. Each time she tried to banish the memory of the feel of his lips on hers, the grinding assault that had turned to a gentle possession, the image of Paulo filled her mind with a disturbing intensity.

After putting on her nightgown, Leigh crawled between the sheets, then fixed the mosquito netting over her. Her attention was drawn to the dark, dancing shadows on the ceiling, shadows that took on the shape of Paulo gazing back at her. Disgusted with herself, she rolled over onto her stomach and shut her eyes.

She couldn't understand her near obsession with Paulo, a man she detested for his arrogance and his condescending attitude. Yet she sensed that under the hardened armor that he presented to the world was a vulnerability, a gentleness that he tried to suppress. He was a complex man, she decided, one she wasn't going to take the time or effort to figure out.

Instead, Leigh forced her attention onto the sounds of the insects and tried to block all other thoughts from her mind. But she failed. Sitting up, she slipped from the bed and put on her robe. She knew it was late and hoped that everyone was in bed, for she needed fresh air and a change of scene without having to worry about defending herself or carrying on a conversation. Easing the door open an inch, she peeked into the outer room and saw that all the lights were out. As silently as a cat, she crossed the living room and escaped onto the veranda. As she breathed deeply of the moisture-laden air, she leaned against the railing, scanning the deserted compound.

A noise at the other end of the veranda made her turn sharply around. To her dismay, Paulo was lounging against the wall of the house with a cigarette in his hand. He placed the cigarette between his lips and drew on it. As he blew the smoke out, he turned toward her.

Leigh folded her arms across her chest and moved toward the door, but Paulo's words halted her. "It's time we had that talk, Leigh."

"I don't think one o'clock in the morning is an appropriate time," she replied brusquely.

"Why can't you sleep?" Paulo covered the distance between them in three long strides. He dropped his cigarette and ground it out with the toe of his boot. "Is it possible you're afraid of what you've gotten yourself into, Leigh?"

"Is that really a question? Or have you already decided it's a fact?"

The laugh lines at the corners of his eyes deepened

as he ran a finger lightly down her arm. "Well then, why can't you sleep? Do the sounds of the jungle bother you?"

She stepped away from his caress. "Perhaps I'm just so excited about the trip that I can't sleep," she told him. "The Amazon has been a dream of mine for a long time."

"Sometimes dreams aren't what you think they are. Besides the constant noise of the jungle, there's the danger of the animals and the insects within it. Not to mention the trip on the river where there are rapids and waterfalls."

"Are you trying to frighten me into backing out? I'm not a quitter, Paulo. I don't go back on my word. And what would you do if I did leave?"

"After this evening, earlier at the river, it wouldn't be right if I didn't give you a chance to back out. I want you to fully understand what's in store for you. One false move could prove fatal, Leigh."

"You needn't worry about me. I'm a big girl now and have been educated in the *perils* that await me." A thread of sarcasm ran through her voice as she mustered all her pride.

The sound of his laughter sent a tremor down her spine. "Contrary to what Marcus believes, I think you'll do fine in the jungle if you heed my warnings and follow my orders without question. If I didn't, you wouldn't be coming along."

A tightness encircled Leigh's throat at the compliment Paulo had given her so begrudgingly. Somehow she knew he didn't give many.

"I won't disappoint you," she said, her voice breathless, almost a whisper.

With just inches between them, Paulo lifted her chin and searched her face for a long moment. Suddenly there were no jungle sounds, only the deafening beat of her heart, as Paulo's mouth descended ever-so-slowly toward hers. She melted against his muscled leanness, her legs no longer able to support her, and wound her arms about his neck as his hands pressed her closer and began to sensually massage her back. She knew she should protest, but she quickly dismissed that thought as his kiss deepened, drawing the last vestige of her strength from her. When he lifted her up into his powerful arms, she didn't object then either. Instead she laid her head on his shoulder, breathing in his musky male scent that filled her with a warmth she couldn't deny.

His arms about her felt so right, his lips on hers felt so wonderful. She knew then she didn't want him to stop kissing her. After her breakup with Frank, she had resisted all male attention. But now she couldn't. She didn't want to.

Paulo carried her through the living room into her bedroom and placed her on the bed. As he looked down at her she felt cold and empty without his arms holding her. She held on to his hand, silently asking him to stay and quiet the disturbing feelings that coursed through her.

"It's late, Leigh. You must get some sleep if you're going to be alert tomorrow. It will be a long, grueling day."

Words formed in her mind but she couldn't say them. She watched him walk toward the door, then he stopped and glanced back at her. "Good night, Leigh."

Then he was gone.

"'Get some sleep,'" she whispered. "But how? You kiss me like that, then order me to sleep. What kind of woman do you think I am, Paulo Silva?"

An hour later she still tossed and turned. Frustration seeped into every part of her, making her muscles tense, her mind full of confusion. Now, when the cold reality of what she had almost done struck her, she bristled with anger at herself—and at Paulo. He had no right to kiss her like that, then walk away. Why did she respond to him so deeply? She wasn't interested in him! She only wanted to do her job. Yet she had practically thrown herself at him, begging him to continue. Never again, she vowed silently. She couldn't afford this seesawing effect on her emotions. No one could.

A sound penetrated her dreamless sleep, causing Leigh to bolt straight up in bed with a start. The knocking persisted until she said, "Yes?" as she scrambled from the bed, searching for the robe she had discarded sometime in the night.

"It's time to get up, Leigh," Paulo called through the closed door.

Leigh inched the door open, her heart quickening at the sight of Paulo already dressed in his tan trousers and white short-sleeved shirt. "But it's still dark," she said, running her fingers through her shoulder-length hair, strongly aware of Paulo's intense gaze taking in her face with a thoroughness that caused her to breathe in sharply.

"I want to push off from the shore at the first sign of light. That means you must be dressed, packed, and have eaten before we even head for the river."

She should have known what his plans were, but every time she was around him and he was looking at her the way he was now, she spoke the first thing that came into her mind. He confused her, he ruffled her usually calm composure. And she couldn't allow him to do it any longer, she told herself as she closed the door and switched on the light.

After quickly dressing, she packed, and then scanned the small bedroom to make sure she hadn't left anything behind. She drew in a deep breath, then released it slowly before opening the door and entering the living room where Jorge and Carlos sat at the table sipping a cup of coffee and eating their breakfast. Sitting down in the chair next to Jorge, she poured a cup full of coffee, then spooned a generous amount of sugar into the strong brew.

Jorge studied her for a moment, then said, "It doesn't look as if you got much sleep, Leigh. You know that's not the way to start this journey." A twinkle of mischief appeared in his brown eyes as he offered her a plate of hot cakes.

Leigh took one look at the food and knew she couldn't eat it; the muscles in her stomach were constricted into a huge knot.

"Don't make two mistakes and start the day on an empty stomach, Leigh. Eat at least one cake and some fruit. You will thank me later." Jorge was dishing up her plate, a smile threatening to break up his neutral expression.

"And what's so funny?" she demanded.

Jorge refrained from saying anything else until Carlos left for the river. Then Jorge swung his amused attention toward her and said, "Eat up. You wouldn't want Paulo to leave without us. Everyone else is already at the river loading the canoes."

Narrowing her eyes, Leigh asked, "Do you know something I don't? You look like the cat that just swallowed the canary."

"Only that I couldn't help overhearing you and Paulo on the porch last night. Did he have to tuck you into bed, Leigh, or was he instructing you in the dangers of the Amazon in the privacy of your bedroom?"

Leigh shot to her feet. "That does it! I don't think it's any of your business, Jorge Bardi."

"And neither do I."

A small gasp escaped Leigh's lips as she whirled to face Paulo, who stood in the doorway with a frown on his face. "I came to see what's taking you two so long. I want to be on our way in fifteen minutes. Do you think you can manage to be at the river in five?" He turned sharply and slammed the door shut, leaving the two of them staring at his retreating figure.

Her features etched with anger, Leigh turned on Jorge. "Isn't it enough that I will have to battle the jungle alongside all of you as well as having to constantly face the hostilities of Paulo and Marcus? Do I now have to fend off your barbed comments, too?"

The teasing look faded from his eyes as Jorge took her hand. "I'm sorry," he said. "I just couldn't resist kidding you about your rendezvous with Paulo on the front porch—at one o'clock in the morning. You rise beautifully to the bait where Paulo is concerned."

"Oh, you're impossible!" Leigh yanked her hand from his, grabbed a piece of fruit from her plate, and headed for the door.

Her strides toward the river were stiff with frustration and anger. She wasn't upset just at Jorge but at herself as well for letting Paulo get to her. Even Frank had never managed to get under her skin as Paulo did constantly. As she neared the river, she stopped to peel the banana in her hand and ate it in four bites, then inhaled deep breaths until her tense muscles loosened.

Now composed, she started for the river again as Jorge caught up with her and walked in silence behind her. When they reached the river's edge, the first rays of dawn were tinting the eastern sky a light gray blue. Paulo was directing the expedition members to their assigned canoes as she halted a short distance from him and waited to see with whom she would ride.

"Place your knapsack in that canoe, Leigh," Paulo told her, pointing toward the second dugout.

As she moved toward it, she suddenly realized that everyone but her, Jorge, and Paulo was in a canoe. At least she didn't have to share a boat with Paulo alone. Thank goodness for small favors, she thought.

As she settled herself between Jorge and Paulo in their twelve-foot dugout. Father Jose blessed the canoes, then lifted his arm in a farewell gesture. The canoe in which

Marcus rode left the river bank first, then Paulo and Jorge pushed off with their paddles and began to maneuver their dugout into the middle of the river. The eastern sky was now a rosy hue with the tip of the sun peeking over the horizon of green.

Listening to the paddles slice through the pea-green water, Leigh scanned the tree-lined banks, marveling at the beauty of the jungle. She knew that behind that beauty lay a savagery that could cause instant death. With all the multicolored flowers that dotted the landscape and the vivid array of birds that nested in the trees, she felt overwhelmed by her primitive surroundings. The heat of the sun touched her skin and she shifted to make herself more comfortable.

It has begun, she thought. With the thrill of a dream come true, excitement flowed through her veins.

But hours later Leigh was no longer excited. Instead, every muscle in her body ached from sitting in the same position for so long. Her clothes felt like a second skin as they lay plastered to her. Sweat ran down her forehead into her eyes, stinging them.

And worse yet, a horde of *pium* had descended on them. Hundreds of tiny, whining flies lit on her arms, ankles, anywhere they could find exposed skin, and sucked the blood from her. She tried to swat at them but nothing discouraged them. Within minutes Leigh noticed small red dots all over her, but she said nothing. She wouldn't give Paulo the satisfaction of complaining. Besides, she saw that he, too, was covered with the same small dots. Let him say something first, not her.

By the time they stopped for lunch and to rest during the hottest part of the day, Leigh didn't think she could move from the canoe. Her legs seemed permanently frozen in a kneeling position. Slowly she climbed from the dugout and would have fallen if not for Paulo's steadying arm about her, supporting her until her legs began to function again. As soon as she felt the life flow back into them, she pulled away from him, his warm touch reminding her of the night before.

Surveying the small beach where they had landed, Leigh noticed some overhanging tree branches that afforded some shade from the intense sun. The shade beckoned to her and she started to move toward it.

"Here, Leigh. Start laying out the food for lunch." Paulo thrust a knapsack into her hands, then turned to walk away.

Lunch? What was she supposed to fix for lunch? She watched Paulo talking to Carlos, then shrugged and opened the knapsack. It contained cans of meat, as well as flour, salt, sugar, and coffee. Was she expected to prepare lunch with just these ingredients?

"Paulo, what am I supposed to make? There isn't much here." Leigh opened the sack for him to see into it.

"Carlos is going into the jungle to get some fruit I saw from the river. With the fruit, manioc cakes, and the canned meat I think we'll survive the afternoon. Start making the cakes and boil water for the coffee."

"Coffee! In this heat?"

"It's either that or plain river water—boiled first, of course. I haven't seen any coconuts yet." There was laughter mixed with his words.

"I know this is ridiculous to ask, but don't you think it's a little hard to boil water without a fire?" Leigh placed the knapsack on the sandy beach.

"One fire coming up." With an amused gleam in his coal black eyes, Paulo clicked his heels together and saluted her before turning to gather pieces of wood.

As Leigh stooped to withdraw the canned meat from the sack as well as the ingredients for the manioc cakes, an intolerable itching began around her ankles. Before she knew it, her whole body felt as if it were on fire. As she collected the water from the river and prepared the dough for the cakes, she scratched herself until the skin around her wrists and ankles was raw. With all her concentration centered around relieving the pain, she didn't notice Paulo's approach. She suddenly felt a viselike hold on her arm, halting any further scratching.

She tried to wrench her wrist away but couldn't. "Paulo!" she cried out.

"Leigh, don't scratch those *pium* bites. You could get one infected and, as you know, an infection can get out of hand very quickly in this climate."

"But what am I supposed to do about this itching? I feel like my whole body is crawling with bugs."

"Grit your teeth and bear it. That's all you can do, Leigh. Up the river a ways there are fewer *pium*."

Leigh knew he was right. An infection in the Amazon, no matter how small it was at first, could become fatal in a very short time.

She watched Paulo for a moment. He didn't touch his bites once! He must be inhuman, she determined. How could he stand there so calmly as if nothing in the world was wrong when she knew his body had to be itching like crazy? Well, if he could do it, she decided, then surely she could, too—*somehow!*

Willing her mind to think of something else, *anything else,* she continued to fix lunch. When it was ready, she filled her plate full and finally sat down in the shade. Under the trees the heat was still intense but at least the broiling sun didn't beat down upon her, baking her unmercifully. She took off her straw hat and combed her fingers through her sweat-drenched hair, then retied it into a ponytail.

Hunger gnawing at her, she cut into a cake and tasted it. Not bad, she thought. With some practice she felt she could become quite good at cooking over an open fire. It was something she had never done, but like all other things she was willing to try to master it.

Taking a sip of her now lukewarm coffee, she winced at the awful-tasting brew and tossed it away. Nothing could convince her to drink that. But what would she drink? Right now there was only the river water and that would have to be boiled and cooled first.

As she finished her lunch, satisfying her hunger but not her thirst, the harsh realities of her surroundings invaded her thoughts. She had read all about the jungle but nothing had prepared her for the boredom of riding in a canoe for hours with only green to look at for miles and miles. Not to mention the insufferable heat, the air so heavy with moisture that it felt like a lead suit pressing in on her. Then there were the insects that never stopped chirping or biting, so many you could never defeat them. In just a few short hours, her nerves were frayed. What would happen to them after a week?

A chattering noise jerked Leigh around and she gasped. A fat, two-foot-long *jacuaru* lizard scampered across dead leaves, finally disappearing into the dense underbrush. Exhaling the breath she had been holding, she relaxed as she saw no further sign of the huge lizard.

"Leigh, if you want to sling your hammock, we're going to be here for another two hours. Then, when the sun is lower in the sky, we'll travel for a few more hours before dusk."

Paulo sat beside her, offering her a smile, silently letting her know that he had seen her reaction to the lizard. There was laughter in his eyes, as if he were telling her she shouldn't have come if she couldn't take the lizards, snakes, and insects. They were as much a part of the primitive beauty of the Amazon as the dazzling flowers.

Well, no animal or *man* was going to make her admit defeat. If nothing else, her experience with Frank had taught her to defend herself, never to allow anyone to put her down, especially because she was a woman.

"That wasn't a bad lunch, Leigh, but the coffee was something else."

"Well, Mr. Silva, from now on you can prepare the coffee." She stood to get her hammock, for she was so exhausted from lack of sleep and the humidity that she almost thought she could sleep sitting up.

Paulo grasped her hand and pulled her back to sit next to him. "Leigh, are you sure you're all right? You didn't get much sleep last night and..."

"I'm fine," she answered in a curt voice.

What was he trying to do? Get her to admit she shouldn't have come? That the Amazon wasn't quite what she had dreamed it was? She would rather suffer silently than say anything to him, even if it was possible that he could help her. Frank had always said that she had too much stubborn pride and she supposed he was right.

A frown chased away the smile on Paulo's face and he spoke in a low voice that conveyed his anger. "Then if you are doing so well, you won't mind cleaning up the dishes." He rose and left without another word.

"Oh!" she ground out between clenched teeth.

As she stood, weariness claiming every part of her, she noticed all the others getting out their hammocks. Leigh hurriedly cleaned up the mess from lunch, using the river water to rinse off the utensils, then found two trees spaced far enough apart to sling her hammock. But as she tried to tie a knot that she felt would hold her weight, she ran into problems. One end of the hammock was fine, the rope caught and held up by a bulge in the trunk, but the other end kept sliding down the trunk whenever she sat in the hammock. As she was searching for another location, Jorge approached, a boyish grin on his face.

"Having trouble?" His mouth quivered with barely contained laughter.

"Yes." Leigh straightened, planting both hands on her waist. "That end doesn't seem to want to stay where it belongs."

"Here, let me fix it for you." He quickly untied the rope and adjusted it so that when she sat down in the hammock it stayed level with the other end.

"Thanks, Jorge. I didn't relish sleeping leaning against a tree trunk."

"I wouldn't suggest it, Leigh. You're much safer in a hammock or in a tree than on the ground. And it isn't me you should thank. Paulo sent me over to rescue you. He said if he came you'd probably refuse his help."

Jorge walked away, leaving Leigh fuming at him— and Paulo. She sought Paulo's smug smile among the men, her piercing eyes stabbing him as if they were two daggers.

As Paulo nodded his head toward her, his dark eyes gleaming in silent laughter, Leigh turned her back on him, muttering to herself, "Don't let him get to you, Leigh Harris. He just wants you to cry uncle."

As soon as she laid her head down, sleep quickly whisked her into a dreamless world. . . . But when she felt a hand nudge her awake, it seemed as if only a few minutes had passed. She didn't want to leave the peaceful, dark world of sleep in which she didn't have to be constantly on her guard. She knew, though, that she must.

Opening her eyes halfway, she stared up into Paulo's handsome face, his expression veiled. In that brief instant while her mind was still clouded with sleep, she wanted to reach up and draw him down beside her.

But that suspended moment was shattered when a teasing glint appeared in Paulo's dark eyes and he said, "Rise and shine. I let you sleep a little bit longer while we loaded the canoes, but it's time to get started, Leigh."

She inhaled a gulp of air, then climbed from the hammock. Facing Paulo, she said in a very businesslike voice, "I appreciate your kindness, but in the future please treat me just like one of the men."

His raking gaze missed nothing as it traveled the length of her, then came to rest on her face again. "You're anything but one of the men, but I'll remember your request in the future."

Her skin felt burned where his gaze had touched her. A slow wave of warmth spread up her neck to cover her face as she looked into the mocking depths of his eyes. Suddenly no one else existed but her and Paulo. As she took a step toward him he reached out and held her hand within his, his thumb stroking the back of it, the caresses playing havoc with her swirling senses. Their mouths were only inches apart when a loud, male voice pierced their haven and Paulo dropped her hand. Marcus approached them.

"We need to get going, Paulo. I want to reach just below the first waterfall by dusk. It's the best place to set up camp."

"Sure."

Paulo started to untie the hammock while Leigh stood motionless, stunned by the realization that, at any time he chose, Paulo could weave a spell over her. No one had ever had this power over her senses before and she didn't like it—even with Frank she hadn't felt like a quivering mass of jelly. And now she was eager to melt into Paulo's arms at the slightest indication from him that he was interested in her!

Bringing her clamoring senses under control, she turned to help him fold the hammock. In silence they walked toward their canoe. When he started to help her into the dugout, their gazes met and a twinkle shone in his eyes.

"Sorry," he said, moving away. "I forgot for a moment you wanted to be one of the boys."

She climbed into the canoe by herself. After positioning herself in the cramped space allotted her, she looked up into Jorge's laughing face.

"Does everything amuse you, Jorge?" she asked, forcing her tone to be light, though she felt anything but cheerful.

"I'm an observer of people, Leigh. It's a fascinating hobby. You should try it sometime."

"I think you do enough for both of us," Leigh muttered as Paulo and Jorge pushed the canoe away from the shoreline.

Again for miles a green ribbon stretched on either side of the green water until Leigh hoped she never saw the color again. She sought and relished the occasional splashes of red, blue, purple, and pink in the treetops that broke the monotony.

About an hour after they had left their resting place, Paulo stopped paddling and handed her his oar. She looked down at the paddle, then up at Paulo with a question in her eyes.

"Since you want to be treated as an equal member of this expedition, it's your turn to paddle. I'll relieve you in an hour." He settled back in the canoe and closed his eyes, his arms folded across his chest. He looked the picture of relaxation in the middle of the afternoon with the blistering sun showering its unrelenting heat down upon them.

The current at this part of the river wasn't swift. In fact, if Leigh had to learn to paddle with Jorge, this seemed the best section of river in which to do so. It was wider here with no sandbars.

Leigh clenched her teeth in determination and sent Jorge a "be patient" look as she began. She plunged the oar into the water and pushed against it but not nearly as hard as Jorge did, and the canoe turned toward the left bank. Quickly paddling, she righted the canoe, then tried again. This time Jorge put less effort behind his stroke and the canoe stayed on course. It took Leigh several miles of paddling before she felt comfortable with her efforts and could ease some of the tension that made her exhausted body rigid. She didn't mind paddling even though she felt the little strength she had regained by taking a nap quickly leave her. But there wasn't anything she could do about that except hope that she could last the whole hour.

Dismissing from her mind all thoughts of exhaustion, insects, and heat, Leigh concentrated on the steady rhythm of paddling that she and Jorge had set. She listened to their oars strike the water at the same time, then forced all her fleeting strength into pushing. She no longer looked at the continuous band of green along the shoreline but instead stared at Jorge's sweat-soaked shirt, watching his rippling muscles as he paddled.

When Paulo finally took the paddle back, Leigh felt numb with exhaustion, her body functioning like a robot programmed to do only one thing.

"Rest for the next hour, then you can relieve Jorge for the last part of the journey today," Paulo said and began the even, strong strokes that moved the canoe at a faster pace.

Relieve Jorge!

She didn't know how it would be possible, but somewhere she would find the strength to paddle again. She was only getting what she had asked for—to be an equal member of the expedition, not to be treated any differently. But it wasn't going to be easy when everything was so new to her. She was a city girl with little experience in camping out.

She soon found herself paddling again, but with Paulo as a partner. Though the minutes had crawled by when she was paddling with Jorge, her hour of rest had seemed to fly at such a rapid rate she couldn't believe it was her turn already.

This time, however, it didn't take long for her to

match her partner's strokes, to keep the canoe in the middle of the narrowing river. The current was swifter in this section of the river, but Leigh was more adept at paddling now than before. Or was it that Paulo and she were more attuned to each other? She didn't know but refused to dwell on that question.

Once the hair on the nape of her neck tingled as Leigh sensed Paulo's gaze boring into her back. She became flustered, missing a stroke and turning the boat toward the shoreline.

Paulo's robust laughter filled the humid air. "We'll never make it to the waterfall for the night if we keep heading for the shore."

She twisted about and glared at him. "Then quit staring at me! I'm doing the best I can. I've never paddled a canoe before. What do you expect? An expert after only one hour?"

"No, but I expect you to turn around and try a little harder. The other two canoes are getting ahead of us."

Never in her life had a man infuriated her so much. She didn't normally lose her temper so fast, but around Paulo that's all she seemed to be doing lately. Leigh attacked the water with her oar, taking her frustration and anger out on it. She was doing a lot of things lately she had never done before. And all because of Paulo Silva!

"At that rate, Leigh, you won't last another five minutes. Slow down." Paulo's mocking voice fired her anger even more.

"What's the matter? Can't you keep up with the pace?" she taunted, then wished she hadn't when she heard his terse reply.

"I said *slow down*. I'm not foolish enough to use up all my energy in five minutes when I have another hour to go. I don't relish having to make camp along these banks."

Leigh scanned the shoreline and silently agreed. Small

cliffs of clay with trees growing out of them lined the river. There was no place to beach three canoes and she didn't really care to help hack out a clearing for their campsite after traveling all day.

After paddling for thirty more minutes, they rounded a bend and found a sandbar stretching across most of the river, making it impossible to continue downstream. Leigh stopped paddling and turned to Paulo.

"What do we do now?" she asked.

"We walk. What else?" Paulo had already started climbing out of the canoe, the water coming up to his knees.

Leigh looked at the murky water and thought about the piranhas and alligators she knew inhabited these rivers. Inhaling in a deep breath, she placed her feet into the warm water and prayed that this river wasn't infested with those creatures.

As they walked along the sandbar, Paulo and Jorge towed their canoe, allowing Leigh to rest the muscles that had begun to ache the minute she had stopped paddling. The water now only covered her ankles, so she could see the bottom. Suddenly a large freshwater stingray that had been half buried in the sand shot out in front of her. Startled, she jumped back, nearly knocking Paulo down. As he steadied himself and her, Leigh shivered at the sight of the stingray's serrated tail which could inflict excruciating pain on an unsuspecting victim.

For a brief moment Paulo rubbed his hands up and down her arms, then whispered into her ear, "Follow us behind the canoe. There may be more stingrays."

His breath on her neck made her shiver even more and she pulled away quickly. However, she gladly followed his advice and was relieved when they resumed their paddling on the other side of the sandbar.

She heard the waterfall before she saw it. The roar grew deafening as they neared it, drowning out the chorus of insects that continuously filled the air since they had arrived in the Amazon.

"How are we going to sleep with that noise?" Leigh shouted above the thunderous sound of the water crashing into the river below.

"I doubt you'll be aware of much noise once you hit your hammock this evening," Paulo answered as they landed on a stretch of beach below the waterfall away from the spray. A nearby path led to the top of the waterfall.

The sky was darkening quickly, the sun now only a golden glow on the horizon as they prepared their campsite. Leigh helped with dinner and greedily ate all of her fish, manioc cakes, and fruit, then fell into her hammock, the blackness of sleep engulfing her immediately.

chapter 6

THEY WERE ON a soft king-size brass bed and Paulo's arms were about her. Leigh could hear his heartbeat pounding against her chest as he stroked her body as if it were a finely tuned instrument. His voice had a deep, velvet quality that charmed her reeling senses. She ran her fingers through the matted hair on his chest, encountering the copper medallion that he always wore. She trailed a finger up the chain, winding her arms about his neck and drawing him even closer.

His breath tangled with hers as he crushed her mouth beneath his, parting her lips and plundering her mouth. His kiss drove the breath from her lungs, his heady male scent arousing her senses like an erotic drug that left her spinning with her need for him. Their bodies met, his hands moving over her with the skill of an expert musician.

This was what she had wanted all along. That undeniable yearning that had begun when she had first met him had surfaced and would finally be satisfied. An exquisite tension was building and building in her as his fingers caressed her into a mindless ecstasy. She grasped those teasing hands and stilled them. She would have no more of that. She wanted him. *Now!*

"Leigh. Leigh!"

Her name filtered through the velvet mist that shrouded her mind, the dream now in a thousand fragments.

No! I don't want to wake up!

But a light stabbed at her eyelids and she blinked. Paulo stood over her, the worry in his expression fleeing moments after she opened her eyes and smiled up at him, her sleep-clouded mind clearing rapidly.

"I had a devil of a time getting you up, Leigh. I don't think I've ever seen anyone in such a heavy sleep."

"Fresh air and exercise can do that to a person. You should try it sometime." Leigh sat up and combed her fingers through her tousled hair, trying to bring order to it but failing.

"You look fine, Leigh, considering this isn't Rio and you aren't going out on the town."

"Listen, I may look as if I've been through the ringer at the *end* of the day, but I refuse to *start* out that way."

"And I thought you wanted to be just one of the boys? Do you see any of us fussing with our hair? Next you'll want to put some makeup on."

"Perhaps some lipstick would help my dry lips. You boys should try it." Leigh rose and, ignoring Paulo's laughter, searched her knapsack for her brush and lipstick. Then straightening, she stretched her sore muscles, rolling her shoulders. Sleeping in a hammock wasn't her idea of a nice soft bed! Her muscles ached more now than they had last night when she fell into her hammock.

"I feel like a naughty girl getting to sleep in. Here it

is dawn and I haven't been up for at least an hour." Leigh glanced at Paulo out of the corner of her eye. "What happened? Did the boss man forget to set his alarm clock?"

"We can all make mistakes. Much to my dismay, when I went to plug in my clock last night I couldn't find an outlet," he joked. "Next time I'll have to remember to use a clock with batteries." After a long pause Paulo continued in a more serious tone. "I saw no reason to wake you up since Marcus was fixing us a delicious meal of manioc cakes and fruit."

"Manioc cakes! I think before this trip is over I'm going to turn into one."

"Well, you'll be thankful that I managed to locate a coconut tree and you won't have to slave over a campfire for drinking water—at least for a bit."

"Oh, and I was counting on fixing coffee for everyone."

He stepped closer to her. "I hope you aren't disappointed that I didn't bother you to make our coffee. I wanted you to sleep as long as possible."

"Paulo, didn't I . . ."

He placed his finger over her lips and stilled her protest. "Shh, Leigh. Let me finish. Only Marcus and I awoke early. Even the other men slept as long as possible. Just like you. We all need to rest as much as we can because of this climate. It has a way of draining all the strength a person has and it can take a long time to rebuild that strength."

Leigh's heart fluttered at Paulo's nearness, at the soft feel of his hand on her arm. She stared into his dark eyes which held a tender expression, and she felt a great pressure against her chest as if that look would steal her last breath.

"I thought you were impatient to get to that Indian village." Words tumbled from her mouth as she stepped back, placing a few feet between them. Her dream was vividly engraved in her mind and she couldn't stop her senses from responding to his raw maleness that seemed to dominate everything around him.

As a bland expression slipped over his features, Paulo flicked his hand toward the waterfall. "Can you see us climbing that steep path carrying our supplies and canoes in the dark? We'll need all the light we can get and then some luck. Marcus says this is the worst waterfall we have to portage, but after this one we still have six more waterfalls and seven sets of rapids. Not a very pretty picture, but one thing is for sure. You won't be bored by the next few days. Yesterday was very sedate compared to what's ahead of us."

Later as they sat down to eat their meal, Leigh was surprised to discover how hungry she was. She hadn't lost her appetite, and asked for second helpings of fruit, coconut, and manioc cakes. She ate as if it were her last meal on earth and would have taken some more fruit if Marcus hadn't started putting everything away, signaling that it was time to begin the steep climb to the top of the waterfall.

Jorge, who was sitting next to Leigh, leaned near her and said, "Well, this is our first big test. Did you see that path we're supposed to use?"

She shook her head. She had been so tired the night before that when they had arrived all she could think of was eating then sleeping. Now she swung her attention from Jorge to the path, and her eyes followed it up the side of the waterfall. The so-called path was little more than a foot-wide clearing of the jungle that ran up the steep cliff, almost a sheer drop, next to the waterfall.

"It wouldn't be so bad if we didn't have to carry all our equipment and canoes," Jorge added. "I haven't been mountain climbing in years."

"I see what you mean."

"This is when you wish you were traveling light."

Leigh found herself wishing that over and over as she clambered up the side of the waterfall carrying three knapsacks of supplies that weighed close to forty pounds. Already her clothes were soaked, her muscles protesting this new torture, but she pushed on, determined to do her part. With a quick glance over her shoulder she saw the strain that Paulo and Jorge were under, towing the canoe up the cliff as well as carrying a backpack each.

Halfway up the side of the waterfall, Leigh's foot caught on a concealed vine and she was sent flying forward. Pain bit into her hand as it struck the tip of a branch lying on the ground, but she didn't allow herself the luxury of tears as she scrambled to her feet and climbed on. With Paulo and Jorge behind her carrying that twelve-foot canoe, she couldn't stop to examine her hand, but the pain subsided to a dull throb so she thought she would be fine. She prayed she wouldn't fall again but it was almost impossible to see where she was going on the path because of the knapsacks she was carrying in her arms and the dark shadows caused by the overhanging tree branches.

When she reached the top of the waterfall, she took deep gulps of air, then collapsed on a rock ledge near the water.

"Did you hurt yourself, Leigh?" Paulo asked with concern as he sat down next to her. Though his breathing was labored, and his clothing drenched with sweat, he showed no other signs of the hardships of carrying a canoe up the side of a cliff in hundred-percent humidity. It wasn't fair! Not when she felt so exhausted and the day hadn't even begun yet!

"Just winded," she rasped as she drew in deep breaths to slow her rapid heartbeat. The fact that Paulo was sitting so close didn't help matters. Every time he came near her, her heart did a wild dance, and she resented the effect he had on her.

"Good. I thought you might have hurt yourself when

you fell. Jorge, Marcus, and I are going back down for the last canoe while the rest of you get everything packed in the other two."

As Leigh watched him leave, she wondered why she didn't tell him about the cut on her hand. But it was small and she could clean it herself while they were below bringing up the third canoe. Opening the knapsack with the medical supplies in it, she withdrew alcohol and bandages. After taking care of her cut, she began to help Carlos, Miguel, and João load the two canoes. They had just finished when Paulo, Jorge, and Marcus arrived with the last one. Their faces were strained and they looked dead tired, but Paulo insisted that the third canoe be loaded so they could leave. There was a lot of ground to be covered that day and still more waterfalls to portage.

Dread settled over Leigh as she listened to Paulo. How could they keep up this rough pace? She wasn't the only one who was tired and in need of a *long* rest.

Again on the river, Leigh took her turn paddling until they met their first set of rapids. "You're not experienced enough, Leigh," Paulo said. "One wrong maneuver and we could all end up in the river. This isn't my idea of a place to take a much-needed bath." He flashed her that disarming smile that could warm the coldest of hearts, then took the oar from her.

When Leigh looked at the set of rapids, she was glad she wouldn't be paddling. They were neither large nor long, but they gave her an idea of what was in store for her later when they reached the really big rapids nearer the Indian village. However, it took all of Paulo's and Jorge's muscled strength to keep the canoe on a straight course, for they were not only fighting the churning water but the current as well.

Yet scanning the riverbanks, Leigh knew why they didn't portage the rapids—there was no place for them to carry their equipment and canoes. A wall of green rose on each side of them with many branches hovering over the river. She saw a long snake draped over one branch, and imagining its beady eyes following their progress, she felt a tightness in the pit of her stomach.

She hadn't realized she had been holding her breath until they were safely on the other side of the rapids and she exhaled slowly, relief washing over her. She hoped they would be able to portage the next set of rapids.

By the time they reached the location that Marcus had picked for the noon rest, Leigh was looking forward to a quick lunch, then a few well-deserved hours of rest. Never in her life had she felt so sapped of energy that she wasn't sure she would be able to climb out of the canoe. Paulo tied it to a tree trunk that jutted out over the water. They were supposed to walk along the tree trunk to the clearing that Marcus and Carlos were hacking out of the jungle.

Leigh extended her hand toward Paulo's so he could help her from the canoe. Suddenly she was thrown off balance as the third canoe crashed into the side of theirs. Both Leigh and Jorge were thrown overboard into the river.

As water engulfed her, Leigh fought her way to the surface. Taking in a gulp of air, she heard the crack of rifle fire and looked up to see Paulo dropping his gun into the canoe and scrambling forward to assist her and Jorge from the river. She grabbed for his outstretched arm and Paulo hoisted her up before helping Jorge out.

Safely on the tree trunk, Leigh stared at the river where she had been only a moment before and saw an alligator being devoured by a school of piranhas. An uncontrollable trembling began in her hands and spread throughout her body. Paulo gathered her to him and she felt a warm cocoon of protection cloak her. She would never forget the white churning water caused by the ferocious fish devouring their prey. And it could have been her or Jorge!

"That was close for you two," Paulo whispered,

smoothing her damp hair from her face.

Leigh heard the rapid thumping of his heart and looked up into his eyes. Did she imagine that his voice had shaken a little as he had spoken? There was nothing, though, in his expression now that indicated it.

Forcing a smile to her lips, she replied in a flippant voice meant to lay her fright to rest, "Well, I did want to take a bath. The only thing I regret is that I didn't take my soap with me. I'll just have to remember to carry it around with me from now on. You never know when the opportunity will arise." Words rolled from her tongue unchecked as she tried to mask her true feelings.

Miguel de Andrade approached Paulo and Leigh. "I'm sorry, *menina*."

Paulo twisted around and lashed out at Miguel. "It takes only one mistake like that one and we have a death in the expedition. Make no more or you're fired."

The steeliness in his voice made Leigh suddenly hope she would never be on the receiving end of his temper again. The anger in his eyes made her feel sorry for Miguel. She'd certainly had her share of that piercing look before and she knew how Miguel must be feeling.

Quickly she said, "That's all right. Accidents do happen. Besides, I was feeling pretty sticky."

Paulo turned his anger on her. "Don't joke about it, Leigh. You or Jorge could have been killed. We can't afford any accidents on this expedition."

"We aren't all perfect like you, Paulo Silva. I was the victim, not you." Whirling, she stalked away from him toward the clearing where Jorge was now starting the fire for lunch.

"That man!" Leigh said through gritted teeth. "You would have thought *he* was the one who went for a swim, not us. He cut into Miguel and threatened to fire him if he makes another mistake."

Jorge looked up from lighting the fire. "Paulo's right, Leigh," he said softly.

"Don't tell me you're angry with Miguel and João, too? The didn't mean it."

"I'm not angry with them, but there can't be any more accidents like that. Next time, Paulo might not be there to save us. Would you have enjoyed being lunch for that alligator? And if *he* hadn't got one of us, the piranhas might have."

"But..."

"There are no buts in the jungle. This isn't a game. Paulo has planned a long time for this expedition and he wants nothing to interfere with its success."

"Oh, I see, and if one of us had been injured or killed that might have interfered with his precious expedition."

"No, that's not exactly what I..."

"That's okay. You don't need to defend your friend to me. I know what kind of man he is." Leigh started to turn away when Jorge caught her hand and stopped her.

In a low voice, almost a whisper, he said, "I don't think you do, Leigh. The hope of finding a drug that could help burn victims is what's been keeping him going since the tragedy that killed his family. He was very close to them. I've never seen him come so close to falling apart, but he didn't because he had this dream. Much like you did about coming to the Amazon."

Her dream. She was finding that she had no time to explore the plant life in the jungle. They were always on the move, eating, or sleeping. There was no time for anything else. Maybe when she reached that Indian village she would have the time. Wasn't that one of the reasons she came? There were thousands of different species of plants in the Amazon and only about half had been identified so far. And only a small percentage of that number had been analyzed, their chemical components determined.

"He isn't a cruel man, Leigh." Jorge broke into her musings. "Paulo is a good, loyal person who would do anything for a friend. But he's under a lot of pressure right now. When this plant is found and we're back in Rio, you'll see a difference."

"But my job will be over by then, Jorge. I won't be around to see this carefree good friend you speak of." Her voice rang with acid, for suddenly she knew she wanted to see that man. She wanted to be around when the expedition was over and they returned to Rio to develop the drug.

"No canned meat for this meal," Marcus announced proudly, holding up the monkey he had just killed.

Turning toward him, Leigh could see the watchful look he directed at her as if he were waiting for her to get queasy and scream at the sight of the dead monkey in his hand. But Marcus didn't know she had often gone hunting with her father. She had seen him kill many animals and had even helped him clean them. However, looking at the monkey, she couldn't help but notice its beautiful, delicate features. She knew she wasn't a hunter at heart.

With a proud tilt of her head she met Marcus's gaze in silence, not giving him the satisfaction of hearing a protest from her. They could eat the monkey but she would eat canned meat or just fruit. She turned way from him and helped Jorge prepare lunch, letting him handle the roasting of the monkey.

When Leigh finally sat down to the fruit, coconut milk, and canned meat, she noticed her surroundings for the first time. On three sides tall trees of mahogany, *imbauba,* and palm towered over her, blocking most of the intense rays of the sun from them like a huge green umbrella. Her gaze swung in an arc, taking in the mass of greenery. Suddenly she spied a garden of orchids growing in one tree. At home she had a small greenhouse where she had cultivated various species of orchids, but they could not compare to what was growing right around her. If only she could pick one, but they were too far up for her to reach, and as tired as she was, she certainly didn't want to try to climb a tree. Sighing deeply, she finished her inspection of the clearing, noting the twisting, tangled mass of vines that often choked a tree. One liana reminded her of an octopus with its many arms wrapped around a tree's trunk, squeezing the life out of it. The law of the jungle was that the strongest survived.

A movement out of the corner of her eye caught her attention and she turned about to watch as Paulo sat down next to her and stretched his long legs out in front of him. His face was still tensed into a frown and she had to silently acknowledge that he might, as leader of the expedition, have a right to say something to Miguel and João. Softening toward him, she broke the silence between them.

"How can you eat that monkey?"

Paulo looked at her tin plate, then at her, his eyes brightening with a smile. "Because we don't have enough canned meat to last the whole expedition. We have to depend on capturing animals along the way. Especially if the journey takes longer than expected."

"I'd have thought you would have brought enough food to last the whole trip. I didn't think you would want to waste time searching for food."

"I had little choice since I had to bring along so many gifts for the Indians. You don't just walk into an Indian village of reformed headhunters without presents. Not even with Marcus having established a good relationship with them. They can still be unpredictable. I've heard too many tales of Indian tribes turning on missionaries for some reason. I don't plan on providing them with one from the beginning."

"I didn't get to thank you for saving my life back there," Leigh whispered, her voice suddenly breathless as Paulo stared into her eyes. She felt he was trying to read her thoughts.

His gaze captured hers in an embrace and she found

herself drawn toward him, his forceful attraction too strong to fight. They were so close that she could feel his breath feather her cheek like a warm caress.

His unwavering look drilled into her, probing, assessing until finally it seemed to find what it was searching for and he turned away, saying in a strangely husky voice, "I was only doing my job."

The brittle pieces of the moment crumbled about her as he spoke those words, not in a harsh voice, but in a voice full of emotion that he was trying to control, to deny.

Standing, Paulo stared down at her as if debating whether to say something, then deciding not to. "Get some rest, Leigh. We still have a long way to go today."

At that moment she knew he felt the almost irresistible pull they had toward one another. But he was fighting it as strongly as she. *Carmen.* He still loved his wife. That's why they were here in the Amazon. When they found the drug, would that free him of his wife? Would the memories still haunt him?

Leigh kept trying to tell herself that it didn't make any difference, but it did. They were worlds apart, brought up differently, believing in almost opposite viewpoints on so many important issues, but it still mattered to her.

Shrugging the confused thoughts away, she fixed her hammock and lay down, placing the mosquito netting over her. She had so many insect bites on her body that she didn't think there was an inch of skin left for an insect to attack, but she wasn't taking any chances. She closed her eyes, and sleep descended quickly.

Leigh cradled her throbbing hand in her lap. The bandage over her cut had been discarded hours ago—it wouldn't stay on her perspiring hand. Looking at the cut, she knew she had better attend to it first thing when they stopped for the night. The skin around the sore was red and swollen, and all she could think about was the consequences of a possible infection. It had only been a *small* cut, cleaned immediately and covered. How was she to realize that the bandage wouldn't stay on, that she would fall into the river? At least one thing was in her favor. They were running into so many rapids and swift currents that she hadn't had to paddle much, just walk carrying three knapsacks through dense foliage.

Leigh pushed a loose strand of hair away from her face. What a day! They had portaged two sets of rapids and three waterfalls. She had gotten to where she dreaded hearing the now familiar thunder of the waterfalls, the hissing of the rapids. That usually meant having to unload everything, then tow the equipment and canoes through the jungle, often making their own path as they traveled with Carlos in the lead cutting and slicing with his machete. Those detours were what ate away at their progress as they journeyed deeper and deeper into unknown territory where the river narrowed and became more turbulent.

Leigh estimated the river was only about a hundred feet wide from bank to bank with tree branches growing over it, blocking out most of the sun. There were even times when they had to paddle under dangling roots, and hanging vines that looked like long, twisting boa constrictors.

The sound of water gurgling, followed by a cuckoo, snapped Leigh's attention back to the present. She searched the surrounding trees for the source and found the oropéndola bird with its four-foot socklike nest in a tree draped over the water not far from them. Then the noise of rustling underbrush disturbed Leigh and she saw a capybara charge out of the jungle and plunge into the river. She kept watching for the large rodent to reappear but it didn't. What had happened?

"They can hold their breath for thirty minutes underwater," Paulo said, glancing over his shoulder at her, but not missing a stroke of his paddling. The constant rhythm Jorge and he had set up continued.

"I've never seen so many animals in one place except at the zoo. And the plants! I wish I had more time to investigate them."

"You will when we arrive at the village." He threw her another look over his shoulder, a frown suddenly furrowing his brow. "What's wrong with your hand, Leigh? It's all red."

Quickly clenching her hand brought a stab of pain shooting up her arm, but it was too late. Paulo had seen the cut and would want to know how it had happened.

Sighing, she answered him. "When I was climbing up the cliff of that first waterfall, my hand hit a stick when I fell." Hurriedly she added, "But I cleaned it immediately and put a bandage over it. It's just that the bandage won't stay on."

"Why didn't you tell me about it then, Leigh?" Paulo had stopped paddling and completely twisted around to face her, his intense eyes boring into her.

"What could you have done that I didn't?" She shot the question at him, suddenly angry at him for thinking she couldn't take care of herself. Sometimes things just happened that people couldn't count on, things that they had no control over.

"I still would like to know about everything that happens on this expedition. When we set up camp this evening, I want to take a look at your hand." Paulo turned back around and resumed his paddling, his voice cold with disapproval.

Leigh had hoped to forget about her throbbing hand until they made camp for that night. Now the pain gnawed at her and that was all she could think of until they turned the canoes into a stream and traveled up it for about three hundred yards. There they set up camp, clearing some of the jungle away so they could have room for a fire and their seven hammocks.

"I want to see that hand, Leigh. Now," Paulo said from behind her, having approached her in silence.

Her heart missed a beat. She whirled and faced him, thrusting her hand toward him. "Here. I was just about to clean it *again*."

After inspecting the wound, Paulo pronounced, "It's infected."

Tugging her hand from his grasp, Leigh said in a voice harsher than intended, "You haven't told me anything I don't already know."

He recaptured her hand, the frown on his face deepening. "I'm going to clean the cut, then give you an injection of penicillin."

Exhausted, the pain of the cut having worn down her good will, Leigh laughed harshly. "Heaven help me if I should delay this expedition with a raging infection. In fact if the infection got worse, you might be forced to turn back and that wouldn't set well with the mighty Mr. Silva."

Paulo shook her; a scowl slashed into his features, then in a too-controlled voice he said, "You're damned right I don't want to turn back after coming all this way, but I wouldn't think twice about it if I had to. If you got that bad, Leigh, have you thought about the fact that you might not make it to the mission? The trip isn't a short jaunt to the local hospital. In this case the hospital is two grueling days' travel through jungle."

Staring into his eyes, she said in a level voice, "*I* will clean the cut," then proceeded to do it.

After Paulo gave her the injection, she started to rise from her hammock. "Stay put, Leigh. Rest," he told her.

"But Jorge could use some help with dinner. Besides, no one can make coffee like me."

"My God, woman, life with you would never be dull. Didn't you ever learn to follow orders?"

"Reasonable ones only, sir." She met his frown with a defiant look.

Suddenly Paulo's frown dissolved into a smile as he laughed. "Please spare us your coffee. I think that's a reasonable request, don't you?"

"I don't think it's that bad since Carlos has shown me how to do it in that contraption you call a coffee pot."

"Do you often have these visions of grandeur?"

"You must be rubbing off on me," Leigh said, amusement in her voice now as she stood. "I'm not an invalid, Paulo. I will do my share of the work, as always."

"Yes. Yes. I should know better by now than to argue with you. A woman can do anything a man can do, is that it?"

"I wouldn't go that far, Paulo. Just as I don't think a man can do everything a woman can do." A twinkle captured her eyes as she walked past him toward the fire where Jorge was splitting a coconut.

But Leigh heard Paulo's robust laugh. "Women! I must have been mad to bring you along."

chapter 7

A LOUD HOWL caused Leigh to bolt upright in her hammock, clenching her blanket to her as her eyes darted around the clearing. The sound reverberated through the jungle and for an instant drowned out the drums that had started yesterday morning and hadn't stopped since.

Leigh realized what the loud noise was and sighed with relief. A howler monkey, down here, just as the rooster back at home, was telling them that it was near dawn. Leigh hugged the blanket to her as the damp chill of predawn rippled through her. She still couldn't get over the coolness of the early morning that quickly evaporated into an unrelenting moist heat.

"I might as well get up and put some more fuel on the fire," she muttered, glancing at the dying embers.

Today they would start their trek into the jungle since

the Indian village wasn't on any river. Leigh wasn't looking forward to it. She knew traveling on foot would be much more demanding than in the canoes, but it also meant they were only about a day's journey from their destination. That excited her.

She stuck some pieces of wood on the top of the glowing embers, then poked at the fire. Small flames began to lick at the sticks and suddenly the fire leaped to life.

She didn't hear Paulo until he cleared his throat, his silent approach like a cat's as it stalked its prey. Was she that prey? Curious that she would think that, but with him she often felt as if she were being hunted. Sometimes it was as if he were waiting for the best opportunity— for what? Leigh pushed the troubling thought to the back of her mind and turned toward Paulo as he sat down next to her.

"Did you hear our alarm clock, too?" she asked.

"I've always been a light sleeper. And I must say a howler monkey isn't my idea of the best way to get up in the morning. I much prefer a soft female voice whispering in my ear." He sent her a look that seemed to say he would like her to be that female.

She looked at him for a long second. A shock of desire rose in her, seeming to match the blaze in his eyes. Quickly she reached for the coffee pot. "I don't know which is worse. The howler monkeys or the constant beating of those drums." Shrugging, she continued, "Oh, well, I'd better start breakfast. To quote our boss, 'We have a long day ahead of us.'"

But his next question made her stop abruptly and turn to look at him. "What are you afraid of, Leigh? These last three days you haven't allowed yourself to be alone with me for one minute. You aren't hiding anything else from me? Your cut is healed, isn't it?"

"I'm not avoiding you," she declared in a louder voice

than she had wanted, a voice that made the words sound hollow, false.

"Then why is it every time I try to start a conversation with you, you find something else to do?"

"Because there is a lot to do. Nobody should know that better than you, Paulo."

"Ah, yes. And you must carry your weight on this expedition." He grasped her hand and pulled her back down next to him, forcing her to look at him. "Leigh, you don't need to prove yourself to me. I think you've done an excellent job so far. As well as any of the others. Stop trying to prove you're better than everyone else here."

Better than everyone else? She had just wanted to stay busy, to keep her mind off the biting insects, the smothering heat, her protesting muscles, and most of all, Paulo. By the end of each day she had no strength left to fight the increasing attraction she felt toward him. So she had just decided to avoid him.

Leigh looked down at their clasped hands and snatched hers away from the exquisite feel of his fingers on her skin. "Is that what you think, Paulo Silva? I don't think I'm better, but at least I'm equal. Every time I turn around I see Marcus's disapproval of me in his eyes. Sometimes he's even shaking his head at something I attempted to do, as if nothing I could do would meet his high standards."

"Why should you care what Marcus is thinking?" His dark gaze narrowed.

"It's not just what he thinks but what you *all* think. I feel as if you all are just waiting for me to admit this is too much for me. Carlos and the others still try to shelter me."

An angry look crept over his features. "Fool, don't you understand that they would shelter anyone, man or woman, who hasn't been in the Amazon before? They aren't treating you any differently than they would any novice to the jungle. So stop pushing yourself."

"But..."

"You aren't going to change my mind about women as a whole. I still think they belong in the home, raising children, making the household run smoothly for everyone. Those are important jobs, too, Leigh. Our society is based on the family, and the woman is the foundation of it, the glue that holds it together."

"Glue! Is that all you think a woman is good for?"

With a bold masculinity that was almost primitive in its force, Paulo seized her and pulled her to his rock-hard chest, imprisoning her slender frame against him. His gaze traced the outline of her lips, slowly, sensuously. She felt as if his potent power had sent a strange lulling current through her and a helpless panic slipped over her.

His mouth was driving in its demanding claim of her, invading her lips to probe the sweetness within, having a devastating effect on her equilibrium. His intoxicating scent fired her, her heart slamming against her breasts so rapidly that she thought she would faint from the swirling sensations bombarding her. Her common sense screamed its warning of the dangers of his seduction and she grew rigid.

Paulo pulled away and stared into the frost of her eyes. "Are you going to fight me every inch of the way, Leigh? You wanted that kiss as much as I did."

"Is that something else you think women are good for?" Her voice matched the temperature of her gaze as she moved out of his arms, away from his reach, and started fixing the coffee, her back to him.

She sensed rather than heard him leave. She made a valiant effort to still the trembling in her hands, but it was useless. He unnerved her as no man ever had.

Leigh had never been so thankful for the presence of the other men as at that moment when she had almost surrendered herself to Paulo. But what if they had been alone? Would she be able to resist his persuasive charm again? She was afraid of the answer, afraid of making another commitment to a man. But then she realized that men like Paulo didn't want a commitment just because they wanted to make love to a woman. And that realization hurt as much as the thought of future rejection.

"You're certainly industrious, Leigh. Up even before dawn," Jorge sang her praises as he poured himself some coffee. "Mmm. And you're getting better at making coffee. I'm impressed. A quick learner."

"Jorge, you're impossible! Can't you ever take anything or anyone seriously?"

An impish look on his face, he whispered, "I bet I'm not as impossible as a certain man we both know—*quite well.*"

Leigh looked at him sharply. "Sometimes I wonder. Why all this baiting?"

Suddenly a serious expression slid over his features. "Because, Leigh, I don't care to see you get hurt. Paulo isn't capable of loving you. Paulo..." His voice trailed off as Paulo approached.

"Haven't you gotten the breakfast ready yet?" Paulo asked as he handed Jorge two coconuts, his voice low, almost a growl. "Make yourself useful by cutting these open, Jorge, while Leigh gets the breakfast ready. It's going to be a long walk today."

Numbly, Leigh went through the motions of fixing breakfast as if she were in a trance. Over and over, Jorge's words filled her mind. "Paulo isn't capable of loving you." She knew that Jorge was referrring to Carmen. That Paulo was still in love with his dead wife. Jorge was just warning Leigh, reconfirming what she had sensed.

After breakfast they packed everything into their backpacks and set out toward the Indian village on foot. As they drove deeper into the jungle away from the river, a strange, forbidding darkness settled in around them even though it was the middle of the day. Shafts of sunlight occasionally broke through the green canopy above and penetrated the dimness of the forest floor.

As Carlos and João hacked their path through the tangled lianas and twisting vines, Leigh surveyed the jungle, now filled with so many different species of plants that it was impossible to count them all. There was no dank or oppressive odor, but the scent of flowers and a fresh humid smell filled the air. More than once Leigh had to suppress a cry when she thought she saw a large snake on the ground that turned out to be the root of a tree. So many of the trees put out root systems above the ground or just under it that she had to look constantly down as she trudged farther and farther into the unknown. She didn't want to repeat the accident at the waterfall where she had cut her hand.

Between her and Paulo she felt an uneasy sense of waiting. More than anything else, she wanted to melt with him in the darkness of sensual pleasure. Yet at the same time she wanted him to recognize her as a woman *and* a skilled botanist with a promising career. With him, though, she couldn't have both, she mused. Lately she felt only confusion, that she was wavering between two opposite poles. Her reason told her to beware while her heart responded wildly to his nearness.

Paulo wasn't the only one of the men who bothered Leigh. Often she would catch Marcus looking at her with a harsh, penetrating stare, his violet eyes a deep purple that made her quiver with the memory of those same eyes gazing down at her from Carmen's portrait. Marcus didn't hide his contempt for her or the fact that he didn't think she had any business on the expedition. But she made sure she gave him little reason to say anything about her performance as an equal member of the team.

Such thoughts rolled through her mind in a jumble.

She was deeply preoccupied with trying to understand Marcus's hostility when suddenly they emerged into a clearing. Her eyes widened at the devastation that lay before them. A whole Indian village had been destroyed; nothing remaining except a few skeletons of huts.

"What happened?" Jorge asked, pushing his hat up off his forehead, his eyes growing rounder at the sight.

"Ants," was Marcus's quiet reply.

Ants! *Army ants!* A hundred-yard strip of jungle on both sides of the clearing had been consumed by these ants which left nothing standing. Though Leigh had read stories about the driver ant, nothing had prepared her for this total destruction.

"Where are the Indians?" she asked in a whisper, almost afraid to hear the answer.

"They fled, no doubt," Paulo replied. "You can hear the ants coming. The sound is horrifying for there isn't anything you can do to stop them. And if by any chance you are caught in their path, there is little you can do to save yourself." He moved into the clearing and turned around slowly.

They all walked quietly across the clearing as if afraid that making a sound would bring the wrath of the ants down upon them. All were sobered to see how such a small creature could destory a lush green jungle in a matter of hours—it was almost as if nature was saying to mankind, "You can't conquer me." They moved on in silence.

Leigh didn't think she would ever get used to the dark gloom of the rain forest with its lofty green ceiling high above her, but by the time they halted for lunch and a rest in another clearing, the sun was high, its intense heat pounding down upon her. The cooler darkness of the jungle seemed a welcome relief that she now longed for as she started preparing the meal.

When she looked up from slicing coconuts, she saw

that everyone was gone except Marcus and herself. Their gazes clashed and Leigh straightened. Alarm nibbled at her but she tried to remain calm and composed as she stared into those hard violet eyes.

"I know what you're trying to do, but you won't succeed, Miss Harris," Marcus said in a low snarl that conveyed his feelings more than his words.

"And what am I trying to do?"

"You're after Paulo. You want to replace my sister's affections in his heart. You won't, though. No man would be able to love another woman after having been married to Carmen. She was beautiful and kind." His eyes narrowed to two slits but remained locked in a silent battle with hers.

Leigh was determined not to be the first to look away. If he was playing some kind of game, he would lose, she vowed silently. But a slight movement above his head caught her attention and she looked up. In a tree branch right above Marcus a snake inched along the rough bark, moving closer to him.

Leigh's eyes widened. A fer-de-lance! Its poison was quick and deadly. And the snake had a reputation for being mean-tempered. She opened her mouth to speak, but fear froze her. Marcus's eyes gleamed in satisfaction at being the victor of the silent challenge he had issued her.

Finally Leigh found her voice. "Don't move," she whispered. "There's a fer-de-lance above your head."

Marcus became paralyzed as he slowly rolled his eyes upward to see the three-foot snake curled around a branch only a foot above his head. No longer mocking, his eyes were wide with fright.

Time stopped. There was no sound, no movement as Leigh and Marcus stared at the snake, both afraid to say anything that might provoke it to strike. Even with the ampules of antivenom in the medicine kit, Marcus's chances of survival if bitten were only fifty-fifty. Not good odds, Leigh thought. But what could she do? Her mind raced with possible solutions.

She surveyed the clearing, trying to think of something to do—anything. A rifle. That was it! She was an excellent shot. Her father had taught her well. Slowly she moved toward the rifle, inch by agonizing inch. Under no circumstances could she alarm the snake.

She slowly lifted the gun to her shoulder and sighted the snake along the barrel. One mistake could mean the end for Marcus; the knowledge was written into his grim features. She held the rifle steady as she squeezed the trigger. *Crack!*

The thud of the fer-de-lance as it hit the ground seemed to echo through the jungle. Relief vibrated through Leigh as she drew in a deep, calming breath.

When she looked toward Marcus, the snake lying at his feet, their eyes again met. She read relief—and something else—in their purple depths. Was it admiration?

The sound of footsteps made Marcus look away, masking his expression, as Jorge and Paulo entered the clearing.

Paulo took one look at the snake and asked, "What happened? We heard the gun but thought that Miguel or João might have shot something for our meal."

"Leigh saved my life," Marcus answered quietly.

All gazes were riveted upon her. Marcus's use of her first name told her she had won a battle with him. For the first time, she smiled, but her nerves were stretched taut as the full realization of what could have happened finally penetrated. Marcus had come very close to death. And death was an integral part of life in the jungle.

Leigh knew she had earned her equal place in the expedition that day, but for the first time she wondered if she would have been safer back home in Kentucky. Her life would be less confusing, less complicated if she were teaching instead of traipsing around a jungle looking for a miraculous plant that might not even exist. Perhaps she would have been better off never having met Paulo and just dreaming about the Amazon. Maybe Paulo was right about dreams. Maybe they weren't always what a person expected them to be.

"Would you like this as a souvenir, Leigh?" Jorge held up the fer-de-lance, its head blown off, for everyone to see.

"Where did you learn to shoot like that?" Marcus asked.

"My father was a policeman. I used to practice at the shooting range with him."

"Well, in the future I must remember to be nice to you. You're some shot, Leigh Harris." Jorge tossed the snake into the underbrush.

Leigh was acutely conscious of Paulo's silence. She slanted a glance toward him, her breath catching at the look of approval in his eyes. Then everything became business again as she finished fixing the meal, Carlos, Miguel, and João having returned empty-handed. They were running low on canned meat, but Paulo thought they would reach the Indian village by late that afternoon. Leigh hoped they would be welcomed.

Later that day her hope was repeated when they found themselves surrounded by warriors in red and black paint, spears raised and pointed toward them. The drums had stopped, and the silence was suddenly eerie, menacing.

Leigh looked from one painted face to another, fear constricting her throat. Her gaze was drawn to a shrunken head dangling from a warrior's belt, and terror engulfed her. Were they really *reformed* headhunters, as Paulo had said earlier?

chapter 8

SEVERAL OF THE warriors circled them slowly, studying them as if they were insects under a microscope. Then the largest of the warriors, who had more feathers in his nasal and ear plugs than the others, spoke to the rest of the Indians in their native language and the warriors seemed to relax, no longer aiming their blowguns and spears at the expedition party.

The large Indian spoke to Marcus, who translated what he was saying to them. "They welcome us to their village. We're to follow them."

When Leigh stepped out of the dark forest into the bright clearing, she was momentarily blinded by the brilliance of the sun. Blinking, her eyes slowly adjusted to the brightness and she was able to survey the Indian village. A massive communal hut stood before her, dominating the clearing, the only structure in it.

Leigh hadn't realized she had halted her step until Paulo nudged her and placed a reassuring hand on her arm. As they started toward the tribal moloka, the monotonous beating of the drums began again, and Leigh wondered as before what message they were sending to other tribes in the area.

When they passed two women stirring something with sticks in a large vat over a fire, Leigh's apprehension didn't recede. She had to place a firm grip on her rising fear and force herself to remain calm while inside she quaked as she watched the women moving the sticks around in slow circles.

She whispered to Jorge, who was walking beside her. "I hope Marcus got it right about them being *ex*-headhunters. I don't think I'd like to be an ornament for one of the warriors."

Jorge chuckled, waving his arm toward the large vat. "Do you think that's dinner?"

"I hope it's their laundry."

They were escorted into the communal hut where all the Indians lived. Leigh was overwhelmed by the sight before her. The hut was over one hundred thirty feet long, seventy feet wide, and forty feet high with a line of glittering fires each belonging to a family that lived in the moloka. Every family had an allotted space to sling their hammocks, but there were no partitions to separate one family's area from the next.

Pitch torches attached to the four center posts of the hut lit the interior. There were no windows, only the opening through which they had entered. Leigh shivered at the flickering, eerie dimness of the huge room, but what made a large, twisting knot in her stomach constrict even more was the mass of warriors standing in front of them. At the front of the throng of Indians stood their chief in primitive splendor. With a proud lift of his head, he stepped forward and waited for Marcus to speak.

Leigh's gaze traveled down the length of the chief's body, taking in his headdress made of macaw, toucan, and parrot feathers, his bark apron, and the necklace of jaguar teeth around his neck. She noticed his dark eyes keenly studying Marcus as he spoke. He was assessing Marcus, a serious expression on his weathered, tanned face, which betrayed nothing of his inner feelings.

As Marcus finished his opening speech, the chief's face split into a wide grin that eased Leigh's tension slightly. But she still felt overpowered by the presence of all the Indian warriors of the tribe massed about the chief, their blowguns and spears in their hands.

The chief shook Marcus's hand, and began a short speech directed at them in his own language. Marcus turned to them and translated. "We are welcomed by Lord Chief Kandi. He is glad to see me again and will help us locate the plant we are looking for. The drums told him of our approach days ago. We are to place our backpacks over there." Marcus pointed toward a vacant place near the opening. "Then we are to greet his warriors and join Chief Kandi for a meal."

Leigh's gaze was fixed on a warrior's waist, where another shrunken head hung from a bark apron. She wanted to shake off the uneasy feeling coursing through her veins, but she felt mesmerized by the small head.

After depositing their backpacks on the hard earthen floor, they moved down the line of warriors. As Leigh stepped in front of each Indian, he shook her offered hand, then gave a short speech. She didn't understand what the warriors were saying, but she shook their hands and smiled anyway. She received more than one penetrating stare of curiosity as they looked at her auburn hair, but she tried to ignore them. These Indians probably hadn't ever seen a person with reddish-brown hair and couldn't help but gawk at her.

By the time she had reached the end of the line, she

thought her hand would fall off from having shaken at least sixty hands, but the smile remained pasted on her mouth as she sat down on a saucer-shaped bench near the chief. She looked out across the enormous *moloka* and was again awed by the size of the hut. In the middle were clustered the women of the tribe, their dark brown eyes as curiously drawn to her hair as the warriors' had been.

At a signal from Chief Kandi, one of the warriors raced to the other end of the long room and brought back a gourd filled with a liquid Marcus told them was *calabash,* a very potent liquor.

"It would be rude to refuse to drink it," he warned them.

When the gourd was passed to Leigh, she took a swallow reluctantly. Not bad, she thought. It was like a sweet-tasting beer, but much stronger.

After the *calabash* had been passed around to the guests, the chief shouted some commands and the women moved forward, laying grass mats at their feet. Huge *beiju* cakes made from the root of the mandioca plant were placed on the mats along with a brownish-colored sauce, which Leigh found out later was a hot mixture that set her mouth on fire as well as her throat and stomach. She gulped down some *calabash,* but the burning sensation died slowly. From then on she ate the *beiju* cakes with no sauce. She enjoyed the rest of the food—roasted fish and peccary with many different kinds of fruit, some she had never tasted before.

As she chewed a delicious piece of peccary, she watched two women lower a large mat over the opening for the night. Suddenly it was as if the world no longer existed except for this tribe of Indians and their small expedition. In all the days of traveling in the Amazon, Leigh had never felt as cut off from the outside world as she did then.

Her gaze wandered around the room, coming to rest on Paulo. He looked up into her eyes, and a smile touched his features, warming her with its brilliant glow. His smile made her feel as if she were the only person in the room who meant anything to him.

But when Marcus spoke to Paulo, he was compelled to turn his gaze away, leaving Leigh suddenly cold, alone in a room full of stangers.

She looked from Paulo to the group of women who were separated from the warriors, serving, tending to the needs of the males. Why was the woman always submissive, the one who served the man? Even here in the Amazon it was no different.

She was so absorbed in thought that Paulo had to touch her arm to get her attention. A shock wave of electricity bolted through her at his caress.

"The chief has told Marcus that if we want to retire for the night our hammocks have been slung for us." Pausing, he let his gaze hold Leigh's for a moment before he continued. "You look tired, Leigh. I think we should take the chief up on his suggestion. If we start early tomorrow, we might even locate the plant by evening and not have to stay here long. I can feel your apprehension and I don't blame you."

"And you aren't afraid of these Indians? Didn't you see that head on the warrior's belt?"

"Yes, to both questions. I would be a fool not to be cautiously wary. These Indians are known for their erratic behavior. The less time we spend here the better."

"For once, Paulo Silva, I'm in total agreement with you."

"Perhaps this is a trend that will continue," he teased. "It would be a nice change not to have to argue with you over everything."

She smiled mischievously. "Don't count on it. I've been known to be very stubborn."

His eyes widened in mock surprise. "How could anyone say that about you?"

"It must be the Irish in me."

He rose and extended his hand to help her up. "I trust you won't be too stubborn about coming to bed now."

"That depends on whose bed."

Paulo laughed. "It would be just like you to say that to me when there are a hundred people surrounding us. You know, I think you enjoy teasing me."

Hooking her arm through his, she lifted her innocent gaze to the smoldering blackness of his and whispered in a breathless, seductive voice, "How else do I keep myself entertained on this trip? I lie awake at night thinking of ways to make your life miserable."

"Well, madame, you've sorely succeeded in your goal. Have mercy on my kind soul and sleep tonight."

Leigh glanced about her, her eyes clouding. "Tonight of all nights I'm not sure I can sleep a wink."

Paulo squeezed her hand. "Don't worry. Remember I'm a light sleeper and will be in the hammock next to yours. In fact, if you want to, we can sling your hammock under mine as the wives of the warriors do."

Ignoring his mockery, she asked, "Have you seen how the Indians have been looking at me? I get chills thinking about it."

"It's your hair. It's like silken fire." Paulo stopped near a hammock slung between two posts and indicated to Leigh that it was hers. "I'll be right here since you obviously don't want to sleep under me." He flicked his hand toward his hammock. "Do try to get some sleep, Leigh. You've been working too hard and this climate is murder on one's health—female and male."

Get some sleep? How could she with Paulo's hammock only a foot from hers and all those Indians so near them? She too had heard stories about Indian tribes turning on missionaries who had befriended them. But when she lay down and placed the netting over her, it wasn't long until the Indians had extinguished the pitch torches and sleep curled through her and sent her into a deep, dream-filled world without Indians. *Only Paulo and herself.*

The sound of voices around her and the feel of eyes boring into her pulled Leigh toward wakefulness. She saw Paulo standing over her with a banana leaf full of food. A smile rested on his features and she had to strongly resist the urge to draw him into her arms and kiss him. The yearning to have his lips possess hers was still there when she sat up in her hammock and placed her feet on the dirt floor.

Paulo handed her the banana leaf and bowed deeply. "Madame's breakfast. I trust you slept well."

Leigh stared at the fruit and *beiju* cakes, then up at him. "Are you trying to spoil me? Breakfast in bed! What am I going to do, Paulo, when I return to civilization and you aren't there to serve me breakfast in bed?" As soon as she had jokingly spoken, she regretted her words, a blush covering her cheeks with crimson. "I mean..."

Laughter bellowed from his chest. "You don't need to explain yourself to me. Enjoy your breakfast. We'll leave right afterward to look for the plant with some of the warriors from the tribe as our escort."

Leigh ate without really tasting the food. How could she have said such a thing to Paulo? But when she had looked into his smiling face she had forgotten their real relationship, remembering only the dream she had had the night before, a wonderful dream filled with love and hope. But that wasn't reality, she told herself as she prepared for the long trek into the jungle.

For hours Leigh followed Paulo, Marcus, and the two Indian guides, who cut their own path out of the dense vegetation. At noon they stopped to eat and rest near an *igapó,* a river that had been trapped inland and formed a lake. Leigh stared across the surface filled with giant Victoria lilies so large that a man could lie down on one.

"Has the Amazon been everything you dreamed of?" Paulo asked easing down next to her on a fallen tree trunk.

"Yes and no. I don't think anything can prepare you for the Amazon. I can't say it has been easy on me."

"I don't believe what I'm hearing!" he cried with mock seriousness.

She leveled a sharp look at him. "But that doesn't mean I can't handle it."

"Of course." A hint of amusement ran through his voice.

"But the plant life is unbelievable. There are ferns twenty feet high and just look at those Victoria lilies. There's no place like this anywhere else in the world, and I wouldn't trade all the hardships I've gone through for anything else you could give me. Thank you for letting me come, Paulo."

Just as he started to say something, a loud squawking noise interrupted him. A small bird was caught in the branches of a bush that looked like a pussy willow. Quickly rising to her feet, Leigh approached the bird, intent on untangling it from the bush, but what she saw made her gasp and draw back against Paulo. The tentaclelike stems of the bush had trapped the bird and were gripping the creature in a death hold that made Leigh shudder.

A flesh-eating plant!

She could see several skeletons of other small animals inside the bush, branches of which were covered with a thick, sticky liquid and suction cups.

She turned from the sight of the struggling bird into Paulo's comforting embrace. "I knew there were plants like this, but it's horrible to see such a large one devouring a little creature. A small Venus' flytrap is one thing, but this..." Shaking her head in disgust and amazement, she drew warmth and strength from Paulo. She hated to pull away but knew that everyone was staring at them.

Masking the quavering in her voice as best she could, Leigh said, "If we're going to find that plant, we'd better eat, then get a move on."

"I know the plant they're taking us to is what we're looking for. Chief Kandi showed me a native this morning who had been burned severely only two months ago. There wasn't a scar on his body."

"Paulo, don't get your hopes up until you have a chance to analyze the plant. The Indians might be exaggerating just to please you. I don't want you to be disappointed."

"I haven't had someone feel such concern for me in a long time," Paulo murmured as he walked beside her.

"Well, then it's about time," she said in a teasing voice while inside she felt anything but flippant. Her heartbeat thumped so loudly that she was sure everyone heard, and her pulse pounded in her veins so rapidly that she thought they would burst.

Paulo looked at her as if he knew what he was doing to her and was pleased by the effect he had on her senses. But Leigh wasn't pleased by the havoc he was causing, frightened as she was to depend on any man. Not after Frank. A man had to accept her for herself and she didn't think Paulo was capable of that. There was no other way, she vowed silently. But at the same time she couldn't deny the clamoring of her senses for fulfillment, the deep yearning within her to be possessed by him.

But why him? She couldn't answer that question. Why was a woman attracted to one man and not to another?

The meal was eaten in silence, the sounds of nature filling the quiet void between them. Then they were on their way again toward the other side of the *igapó* not far from the lake.

When they finally found the three-foot-high fernlike

plant, Leigh could barely contain her excitement. She had never seen anything like it. It had broad, deep green leaves with stems that burst from the plant's base like tentacles on an upside-down octopus.

Leigh worked quickly cutting the plant. When she was finished she repotted it in a large container they had brought, hoping the plant would survive being uprooted from its home. She filled the container with soil from the area. That would help it's chances of surviving the trip to Rio, but nothing was guaranteed. Yet Leigh felt confident. She had a sample of the plant to study as well as samples of the soil it grew in and cuttings that she hoped would root and become full-fledged plants. Still, there was no quick way to tell if this plant was what Paulo dreamed about. It had to be analyzed and that would take months.

As they headed back toward the Indian village, Paulo walked slightly behind her. She could feel his eyes on her and turned to look at him. There was excitement in his features, but a trace of doubt creased his brow.

"What do you think, Leigh?"

"It's hard to say, Paulo. I've never seen a plant like this one. It's a fern, but nothing like what we have in the United States. But then, the Amazon is full of new and different species."

"Chief Kandi is giving me a sample of the paste they make from this plant to take with me." He chuckled. "In exchange for a beautiful, shiny machete that I just happened to bring along with me. He was like a little boy in a toy store when he saw all the things I brought as gifts for him and his tribe. These Indians are so isolated here, but . . ." Paulo's voice trailed off at the sadness of what would happen to the Indians when so-called civilization caught up with them.

"I've read about what's been happening in other parts of the Amazon," Leigh said. "Whole tribes almost wiped out from contact with the outside world."

"They are a strong race, but they aren't used to our diseases. Common illnesses we recover from in a few days can be extremely serious for them. A simple flu can kill half of a tribe in a few weeks."

After they returned to the communal hut and Leigh had carefully taken care of the plant and the soil samples she had obtained, she lay down in her hammock. She would close her eyes just for a minute. Even after traveling for six days to reach the village she was still tired from walking so much today.

"You would think I would be used to it by now," she muttered, but her sore muscles told her otherwise.

Closing her eyes, Leigh listened to the sounds of the Indians in the hut, the noise quickly fading as sleep claimed her. It seemed as if only a few minutes later Paulo was shaking her awake.

"Time to get up. I allowed you to rest for an hour, but you have to join the feast the Indians have prepared in honor of our success. I'm ready to celebrate."

Paulo pulled Leigh up to a sitting position, her mind still shrouded with sleep. His touch sent flames of fire across her skin and the loud activity around her fully wakened her.

As her eyes focused on him, she drew in a quick breath at the cluster of orchids in his hands. He held the flowers out for her to take.

With a brilliant smile softening his chiseled bronze features, Paulo said, "I couldn't resist these. They would look perfect in your hair. A gift from an admirer."

Speechless, Leigh just stared at the orchids. The petals were cream-colored with red veins running through them. They were the most beautiful orchids she had ever seen. Were they beautiful because Paulo had given them to her? Yes, she decided silently. She knew she would cherish anything he gave her. This tender gesture touched her heart and made it throb.

"Leigh."

The gentle way he said her name cascaded over her in waves of warmth that caused her heart to quicken its pace. She lifted her gaze to his and whispered, "Thank you, Paulo. They are beautiful. Orchids are my favorite flower. When we're traveling through the jungle and I look up and see wild orchids growing in the trees, I don't feel nearly as bad. They are a refreshing sight—one of nature's wonders."

Something flickered in the dark depths of Paulo's eyes. Desire? Satisfaction? She couldn't tell for he quickly masked the fleeting expression.

"Well, madame, we have a party to attend. And since you're one of the guests of honor, I suggest you hurry. Personally I wouldn't mind a stroll in the moonlight alone with you, but I think Chief Kandi would be disappointed if we failed to show up. I think he's taken a fancy to your red hair. Don't be alarmed if he wants to touch it."

A blush tinted Leigh's cheeks as she gazed at Paulo. His eyes told her the chief wasn't the only one who wanted to touch her hair. In that instant she became shockingly aware that she wanted this waiting between her and Paulo to end—*that night*.

She stood up, and after brushing her hair, placed the orchids behind her right ear, their delightful aroma teasing her senses. From across the enormous room she heard the deep pulsating sound of the drums as they signaled that the feast was about to begin. With a glance toward the door, she noticed that dusk had turned into night, the sky black and clear, filled with twinkling stars.

"Marcus has informed me we'll get to see the dance of fertility tonight. It will be a treat, don't you think?"

Paulo's mocking voice sent chills over Leigh as she met the devilish glint in his ebony eyes. "Yes. I've read about the dance," she answered in a matter-of-fact voice that didn't betray the turmoil raging inside of her.

Paulo threw back his head and laughed. "That seems

to be all I've heard lately. What did you do before coming on this trip? Lock yourself in your room and read twenty hours a day?"

Leigh giggled. "You know, I think I should write my own book on the Amazon. With all I've learned on this expedition and with all the books I've read about the area, it would be quite informative."

As she sat next to Paulo on the saucer-shaped bench, she watched the warriors smearing red paint over their bodies, then drawing beautiful designs in black paint with small twigs. Their bodies glistened in the firelight as they prepared for the feast. Leigh's attention swung from them to the women of the tribe and she had to suppress a bitter laugh as she observed them squatting on the dirt-packed floor watching their men decorate themselves. The women would wear neither paint nor adornments. The men took all the glory while the women contented themselves with remaining in the background doing all the work.

When Chief Kandi approached them, Leigh marveled at the majestic bearing of the proud Indian who wore a beautiful feather headdress and carried a decorated shield and spear. His body was also painted red, but with a blue design that was a work of art. He brought his spear down on his shield and suddenly the feast had begun.

The warriors started to sing and sway to the music, a provocative rhythm that filled the huge moloka with its pulsating beat. A few of the Indians were playing the music, using reed pipes, several types of flutes, some a foot long, and of course the drums that Leigh had finally grown used to hearing most of the day. It was their way of communicating with other tribes, but it was also a distressing, somewhat menacing sound. To complement the music many of the warriors shook rattles as they formed a wide circle and moved slowly around it, stomping their feet and shouting.

As the tempo of the music increased, the men began to twist, stamp, and undulate their bodies, their movements wild and intense. Their elongated silhouettes danced on the ceiling in the eerie firelight, making them seem larger than life.

A momentary jolt of fear streaked through Leigh as she watched their shadows strike the ground with their clubs. She must have outwardly shown some sign of her fear, for Paulo placed his arm about her shoulder and drew her closer within his protective embrace. All fear vanished as she felt the warmth of his body radiate through hers, filling her with a glow of contentment. She was safe with him next to her.

Next, the women of the tribe joined the men; the tempo slowed again and the men and women locked arms about each other's waists and began moving in a circle around the fire. The Indians were no longer wild and primitive in their movements, but solemn and reverent. Impressed, Leigh became mesmerized by their gentle rocking. It was as if they were trying to hypnotize her, and bit by bit she felt them succeeding as Paulo's hand massaged her upper arm. When the music ended and the warriors pounded the earth again, she released a deep breath and shook her head to rid herself of her dazed feeling.

She was starting to relax as the women began serving the food. There were different kinds of fruit, the usual *beiju* cakes with the hot sauce that Leigh avoided, turtle eggs, roasted turtle meat, roasted paca, and several types of fish. Indeed a feast! Leigh sampled everything, including the turtle meat which she found the Indians especially liked. But her favorite dish was the roasted paca, its flavor tasty and tantalizing.

"I can't believe I've enjoyed eating this paca so much. It's a rodent, but so delicious," Leigh said to Paulo between greedy bites of food. The long walk earlier in the day had given her a ravenous appetite.

"The animals they hunt are strange to your country," Paulo said, flashing his disarming smile, "but the animals you eat would be strange to them."

When he smiled at her that way she thought she would melt into his arms in front of everyone in the moloka. Wouldn't that be a sight! And before the fertility dance even began. Leigh laughed silently at the thought.

"Since I landed in Brazil, I've eaten almost no American food. I'm going to forget what a hot dog or hamburger tastes like."

Paulo's disarming smile dissolved as his gaze caught hers in a steely snare. "Are you in such a hurry to return to the United States?" His words were spoken softly, for her ears only, with just a hint of coolness in them.

"Yes—no."

His steadfast look unnerved her, scattering her thoughts. She was powerless to do anything but look into the swirling darkness of his eyes as they gripped hers in an invisible hold. Silently they shared an intimacy with a hundred people laughing, talking around them. For that moment there was no one else in the communal hut but Paulo and herself.

He lifted his hand and touched her cheek tenderly, then trailed his fingers down to her chin. She tore her gaze from his and studied the earthen floor. Shaken to the very core of her being, she tried to mask the turbulent feelings visible in her eyes. She had never been good at keeping her true feelings secret, and this time was no different. She was as unsettled over the look he had given her as she was over the gentle caress that had unleashed a wild, shaky excitement within her. Her spine tingled with anticipation. *Anticipation of what?*

Mercifully, she didn't have to answer that question as the music started again and Indian couples began forming a circle, alternating man and woman. In the center of this huge circle, stood a young woman with a baby in her arms. As the Indians, clasped arm in arm, moved to the sound of the music, the warriors shook their rattles and some of the men threw red seeds over the dancers.

Leigh was moved by this beautiful offering in the form of a dance, this poetic gesture. Only by giving birth to lots of strong, healthy children could the tribe hope to survive as a race. With the modern world intruding more and more into their lives, the odds were against them. Leigh wiped a tear from her eye at the thought.

Suddenly the walls of the moloka seemed to be closing in on her. She had to escape this stifling atmosphere. Her nerves were taut with apprehension. Her world was falling apart, it seemed. One look from Paulo and she would no longer belong to herself. Slowly, little by little, she was becoming dependent on him for something. But what? she asked herself. Love? Physical release? *What?*

When the dance ended and everyone became absorbed in talking and eating, Leigh saw her moment to escape. She rose quietly and walked toward the opening, grabbing the blanket from her hammock as she left. Removing the orchids from her hair, she fingered one petal and headed away from the noise.

She felt a weight lift from her as she escaped into the dim night, the bright moon, illuminating her surroundings in silvery radiance. The beating drums invaded the quiet of the compound outside the communal hut, but the sound no longer hammered so insistently inside her head.

As she put more distance between herself and the tribal moloka, the tension that had knotted her muscles slipped away and she relaxed for the first time since coming to the Indian village. The soft sounds of the night mingled with the constant beat of the drum, making the drum seem less menacing and more erotic as she sat on the blanket she had brought and listened. The warriors' chantings floated on the light breeze that combed through her hair sending veils across her face. As she looked up at the velvet sky, she closed her eyes and wished on the first star she saw.

"I hope this plant we found is the answer for Paulo," she whispered aloud.

The cluster of orchids Paulo had given her lay in her hand. Her favorite flower, she thought. *And somehow he had known.* There were times when she felt he could read her thoughts, that he knew everything about her.

Leigh relived the moment when he had handed her the orchids, feeling again the lump that lodged in her throat, choking off all words as she stared into his compelling black eyes.

She hadn't thought such gentleness possible in a man like Paulo, a ruthless man who took what he wanted when he wanted it. But the tenderness in his eyes had reached into her very soul and touched it like a lover's caress. She felt bound to him now, bound in some inexplicable way that frightened yet excited her.

Running a finger lightly over a velvet petal, she tried to rid her thoughts of Paulo, to forget for a short time the man who had lately become so much a part of her thoughts. But his image stayed in her mind, his smile still enticed her, sending her senses soaring.

When she heard footsteps approaching and looked up to see Paulo nearing her, she wasn't surprised. She had known he would follow her. She had wanted him to. *The waiting was over now.*

Paulo sat down next to her on the blanket without speaking. There was no need for words. It was as if this meeting had been ordained from the beginning and nothing Leigh could have done would have changed it. Paulo took her hand in his and held it in silence as they stared into the black jungle for what seemed like hours but was actually only a few minutes.

"You knew I would come, Leigh."

The seductive pitch of his voice flowed over her, wrapping her in a warm cloak. She felt protected, safe from the world as he enfolded her into his embrace.

"You wanted me to come."

She didn't respond to his statement. She didn't need to. Instead, she wound her arms about him and drew him even closer, pulling his hard, muscled body to hers. The feel of him so close, his heady male scent causing her senses to react as if they were a runaway train speeding down a hill with no hope of stopping, released Leigh from the restraints she had placed around her heart. She was free, totally alive as Paulo pushed her back onto the blanket and fitted his long body to hers. His warm mouth teased the delicate skin of her neck and earlobe.

Her senses were heightened with an awareness of every small movement of his hand over her skin, of his lips on hers, and she found herself returning each caress with one of her own, matching each kiss with the same intensity.

Nothing mattered to her but the blissful sensations that spread through her like molten liquid and the strong longing that screamed its need for fulfillment. Her breathing became ragged when his hand cupped her breast and caressed it gently in slow, sensual circles that left the burning brand of his possession on her.

When his mouth drew the last trace of doubt and resistance from her, they met, coming together in a world dominated by their need for each other. Leigh felt as if hundreds of tiny explosions were igniting within her. When she thought she had climbed to the highest plateau of ecstasy possible, he pushed her higher with his tantalizing kisses and the rapturous feel of his flesh against hers.

Afterward, as they lay in each other's arms, a curtain of darkness shielded them from the world. Leigh tried to bring order to her riotous thoughts, but the memory of their union left her intoxicated with his raw sensuality. Nothing had felt so right as his arms about her or his lips on hers, demanding, seeking.

But as the delicious feelings slowly evaporated with Paulo's continued silence, doubts intruded. What now, Leigh wondered, gazing at the star-studded sky. As she listened to his ragged breathing become deep and even, all her former uncertainties returned to plague her, making her draw slightly away from him.

"Leigh." He whispered her name in a deep, husky voice intense with emotions.

She waited for him to continue; she could not speak. Seconds dragged into a minute before he continued in a more level voice. "I don't want you to go back to the United States when this is over. Will you stay and work on the project with me in Rio? I need a good botanist."

Stay in Rio? She had longed to hear those words, yet now she wasn't sure if she should stay. Would she be yielding the last of her independence? For she knew instinctively that if she worked for Paulo they would be more than employer and employee. They would be lovers. Did she want more? Her head throbbed with confusion. She was torn between the securities of her old life and the uncertainties of the new one he offered her, wanting both desperately.

Why couldn't she have both, she asked herself. *She loved Paulo! And she loved her independence, her career*.

She and Paulo had just made love. She no longer had to fight her love for him, or deny it to herself. Her answer was clear.

"Yes, Paulo. I'll stay and work with you," she whispered as his hold on her tightened.

His lips demanded an awakening of her senses again and gladly she gave it. But as they came together, a small seed of doubt remained. *What of Paulo's feelings? Did he still love Carmen? Could he love again? How could he make love to her like this and not feel something?*

As his hands wove a magical spell over Leigh, she pushed these doubts to the back of her mind. She would have time in Rio to discover his feelings.

chapter 9

LEIGH STARED AT the rushing green water, going over in her mind the events of the last two weeks, reliving the feel of Paulo's lips on hers, his body next to hers. She would never forget that night after the Indian feast when she had given herself up to him. Now they were back at the mission and would be returning to Rio tomorrow. Excitement and fear mingled within her to make her uncertain of the future. Yes, she would work with Paulo in Rio. But then what? That question had haunted her all the way back to the mission.

All they had shared since that night had been glances and a few kisses that had left her feeling empty, not quite sure of the future. His intimate smiles warmed her, but she needed his arms about her. She wanted to hear words of love whispered in her ear.

Her love for him grew each day she was near him as she continued to see glimpses of his tenderness and kindness. He wasn't the ruthless man she had at first thought him to be. He had a driving need to help others, to make their lives less painful. He loved his work as a chemist and enjoyed running his pharmaceutical company.

"There you are." Paulo's deep voice cut into her thoughts.

She turned and was enveloped in his embrace. "I had to say good-bye," she said. "This has all been quite an experience."

"Sad you're leaving?" he whispered, his voice muffled by her hair.

"No. Most people never get to fulfill their life's dream. I did. This place was everything I imagined it to be in the way of plant life. I'm glad you let me come."

"I never thought I would be saying this, Leigh, but I was wrong about you. You were a real trouper. You did as good a job as any man."

Leigh stiffened and pulled away. "I think that was a compliment, but I don't like the sound of it. Why shouldn't I have done a good job? Women are capable of doing good jobs, too."

"In some jobs."

"You haven't changed your pigheaded opinion one bit, have you? Whatever made me think you would?"

"Here we go again. Women can do anything men can do, is that it?"

"Yes—I mean, no. I will admit there are differences between the sexes, but women have as much right to a career as men. Women are just as smart and capable of running a large corporation, of being a scientist, a doctor, or anything else that they are trained for."

Without a word Paulo turned and began walking toward the mission. Infuriated, Leigh balled her hands into fists at her sides. Just as she thought he was softening his narrow-minded view toward women, she was proven wrong. Would they ever agree? Would they always fight about it? She couldn't see having a lasting relationship with a man who denied her her own identity as a person. It was just as important to a woman as it was to a man. Couldn't Paulo see that? Yes, she wanted to be a wife and mother, but that wasn't all. She couldn't exist simply to please others, to be always at the beck and call of her family. There was more to life than that—wasn't there?

She stared at Paulo's retreating figure, her anger making her back ramrod straight, her features strained. How could she go back to the mission and act as if everything was fine? How could she stay in Rio and be so near Paulo, yet so far away? Again she was reminded of the differences in their backgrounds. They had been raised in two different cultures. Could they ever meet in the middle? Could they compromise? Leigh's doubts resurfaced and gnawed at her composure.

"Hello, Leigh. Paulo told me you were down here," Jorge said cheerfully, too cheerfully. "You two must have had a fight. He didn't look very happy."

"You might say we had a disagreement."

"What did you say to him? Not thirty minutes ago he was on top of the world. He was so excited about getting back to Rio and starting the work on this drug. He was as he used to be before the fire."

"We didn't see eye to eye on something, that's all."

Jorge stood next to her, his arm touching hers. "Leigh, be careful. Paulo told me this morning that you agreed to work with him on the drug. You can't change a person overnight, if ever. Don't expect a miracle where Paulo is concerned. He's what he was molded into as he grew up. He's a very stubborn man."

"In other words you think I should leave Rio, get away from Paulo before we both end up hurt and disappointed." Leigh faced Jorge with pain in her eyes.

"That's easier said than done. I wish I could walk away from this expedition and never look back, but I can't. I've been standing here trying to convince myself to leave. *But I can't!*" Tears misted her eyes. "Oh, God, I wish I could."

Jorge placed a comforting arm about her shoulders. "I know I've teased you in the past, but if you ever need to talk, I'll listen. I might not be able to help, but I'm a good listener, or so the ladies tell me."

The lightness in his voice chased away her sadness and she laughed. "And I bet there have been a lot of ladies."

"Oh, just sixty-seven, but then who's counting?"

His laughter-filled reply made her momentarily forget her worries, her doubts. The sun was sinking in the west, dusk rapidly approaching. "We'd better head back to the mission. I don't want to be caught out here after dark without a flashlight."

She vividly remembered the last time she had escaped to the river and dark had descended quickly, leaving her to find her way back without a light. She imagined again the bruising kiss Paulo had given her, the one which slowly turned into a gentle possession.

That was when she started loving him.

"Yeah. I almost forgot I was supposed to bring you back for the tour of the hospital that Father Jose wanted to give you."

"You're some errand boy, Jorge. You can't even remember why you were sent to fetch someone."

They hurried toward the mission as the bright light of the sun dulled into the shadows of dusk, the trees casting the path in dimness. Things would be different when they returned to Rio tomorrow. Paulo would be on home ground, back among familiar surroundings while she was still miles from home, unaccustomed to his life style, to his culture. Would her love turn to hate, frustration? Was it strong enough to weather the storm she felt was brewing?

When she reached the hospital, she greeted Father Jose with a smile, saying, "I'm sorry I'm late. I was saying farewell to the Amazon."

"This place can weave a strange spell over a person," Father Jose agreed.

Much like Paulo had woven a spell over her, Leigh thought as she followed the priest into the hospital.

Throughout the tour, she couldn't keep her mind on what Father Jose was saying. Instead she went over and over what Jorge had warned her about. Did she want to change Paulo, make him into a different man from the one she had fallen in love with? Perhaps subconsciously she did not want to have a permanent relationship with him. Maybe that's why she and Frank never married. Had her parents' broken marriage influenced her at an early age?

By the time Father Jose had finished with the brief tour, Leigh's head pounded with her unanswered questions. If only life could be simple, uncomplicated. By coming to Brazil she had jumped from a fire into a raging inferno that was sure to leave her burned, with scars to carry with her for the rest of her life, scars that no medicine could cure.

When she returned to the small white house where the rest of the people were gathered for dinner, she didn't feel hungry. Her emotions were too raw, her heart painfully hammering against her breasts as she looked into Paulo's angry eyes. Love was forcing decisions on her that she wasn't emotionally ready to make. Frank was still too fresh in her memory.

As the meal progressed, Leigh was repeatedly thankful for Jorge's cheerfulness. He kept the conversation flowing around her, the topics always safe ones. She couldn't help but notice that Marcus wasn't as hostile toward her as the first night that they had sat around this same table. He wasn't friendly either, but she didn't have to defend herself in his presence or try to ignore his lancing stares. At least she had won a small victory with him when she had shot that snake. Why couldn't she win the war with Paulo?

Later that night Leigh again found herself drawn to the porch. Restless, she slipped from beneath the netting and put on her robe. This was her last chance to enjoy an Amazon night, a night filled with sounds of animals and insects, but a strangely comforting darkness that engulfed her in a world where there were no outside, civilized worries to bother her. Where the next paycheck was coming from didn't matter here. Material things had little significance in the jungle outside of the necessities that kept a person alive. Life was stripped of its adornments. Only one's basic needs counted in this tropical climate.

Stepping onto the porch into the warm night air, Leigh leaned against the railing and drew in a deep breath of moisture-laden air. She thought back to their harrowing experiences on the rapids coming downstream, the exhausting travels around the more dangerous rapids and waterfalls. Although the trip had been physically exhausting, it had been mentally invigorating. She had known what to expect on the return trip and had enjoyed it more. Now it had ended. Would her relationship with Paulo end too?

Footsteps filtered into her thoughts and she swung around to face Paulo. She had half expected him to appear; she had secretly wanted him to appear. But why? To reassure her that she was making the right decision by staying in Rio? She wanted to feel close to this man, who was neither smiling nor frowning. She *needed* to feel close.

"You couldn't sleep either," she said.

"You knew I would be here."

Leigh felt uneasy. He had such an uncanny way of reading her thoughts. It was as if they were one person instead of two separate identities. And that was what unsettled her the most. She no longer felt like Leigh Harris, a botanist from the United States. But neither could she grasp what she was becoming.

"I don't like us parting as we did at the river," she finally said when the silence had become unbearable.

"I think we have exhausted that subject. You don't want to change and I can't."

Before she realized it, her anger had taken over again. "And I'm supposed to do all the changing." She turned sharply to leave, but his hand on her arm stilled her flight.

"Leigh?" There was a pleading tone in his voice that calmed her.

"Yes?"

"Must we fight? I just want to hold you. The expedition has been a success, yet something is missing. Won't you share this victorious moment with me?"

Her anger disappeared as his soft, soothing words cascaded over her. How could she refuse him? She wasn't sure she could *really* refuse him anything. She felt powerless in his presence and that frightened her. *He would win in the end!*

But in a teasing voice she said, "You don't think our arguments add spice to your life? I have a friend who loves to pick a fight with her husband just so she can make up. She says life would be boring if they didn't have a fight at least once a week."

For the first time that evening a genuine smile crept over his features. "I like the part about making up. Let's try it."

"You mean, Paulo Silva, that's what you've been doing? Why didn't you tell me you just wanted to kiss me?"

His mouth made an unhurried descent toward hers, his fingers entwined in her hair. Just an inch from her mouth he paused, prolonging the delicious moment before his mouth claimed hers. He brushed his lips across hers so lightly that a tingling sensation shot down her spine; then he whispered, "I'll remember in the future."

All the defenses she had tried to erect against him crumbled rapidly about her feet. She couldn't fight the sensual arousal that he was expertly orchestrating. Not when his hands were molding her to his hard contours, when his mouth was drawing a passionate response from her that left her breathless but wanting more—much more.

"Oh, Paulo, why *do* we argue?"

His mouth was now trailing a path of teasing kisses to her earlobe. "Because we're so different. But that too can add spice."

She wasn't sure about that. Not after Frank. But with Paulo nibbling at her earlobe she didn't care whether they were different or alike. The only thing that did matter was that he continued.

As he tantalized the sensitive skin of her neck, a velvet mist shrouded Leigh, her mind spinning from the caresses of his mouth and hands. She clung to him in desperation, wanting to feel every inch of him, wanting to make him a part of her.

But without warning he tore away from her, leaving her abandoned, betrayed. "Someone's coming," he muttered, just loud enough for her to hear.

She composed herself, then searched the darkness, but didn't see anyone. Then Father Jose appeared from the dark shadows and mounted the steps to the porch.

"Good evening. I didn't think anyone was still awake. I had an emergency at the hospital," he informed them.

Leigh gritted her teeth. This sense of helplessness, of having no control, were what made her feel that she was incomplete without Paulo. It was as if he were her other half. Even with Frank she had felt separate and independent. She knew she could make it on her own. Now she wasn't sure. A world without Paulo seemed dismal, unreal.

"Good night, Father," Paulo said as the priest entered the house. Paulo turned back to her, his expression hidden by the night shadows.

In the silence Leigh felt that the intimacy of their previous moments together was gone, not to be recaptured that night. This was neither the time nor the place to fulfill their yearnings.

"The worst part of the trip back to the mission was being so near you, yet not being able to hold you, to make love to you." Paulo stepped closer until their bodies touched. "When we arrive in Rio, will you stay in my guest house on the estate?"

Leigh wanted to say yes, but common sense told her to say no. Shaking her head, she moved back a step, putting as much distance between them as possible. She didn't think she was ready to surrender completely to him, though in her heart she already had.

"Leigh, my lab is in my home. It would be easier if you lived nearby. You would have your own place near the entrance to the estate. You could come and go with a car of your own. I want you near me as much as possible. Please, Leigh." His arms wrapped around her and crushed her to him. He nuzzled her neck, spreading chills over her flesh.

Common sense fled when she was in his arms and he knew it. He was using his effect on her to get his way now, and she couldn't do anything about it. She found herself whispering the word yes as if her lips had a will of their own.

She knew she was lost as she gave in to the passionate thrill that roared through her.

chapter 10

LEIGH LISTENED TO the pounding surf as she stared at the azure water. This was *her* secret place to escape to when she'd had a particularly bad day or a fight with Paulo over the phone. One day, though, she would bring him here and share this beautiful, secluded beach with him. She had been lucky to find it since beaches in Brazil weren't privately owned. But for some reason, probably because it was outside Rio, no one else came here, at least not while she had been there.

She sat on the sand and released a deep sigh. Two weeks! She had been back in Rio for two weeks, yet it seemed as if she had been here always. Rio was in her blood now—as was Paulo.

She could remember as if it were yesterday moving into the guest house, the size of her mother's home back in the States, with Paulo planting a kiss on her lips, then leaving her to rest. She had awakened from the long nap and gone up to the main house. Everything since then seemed like a nightmare. First Paulo had left for a two-week trip to Europe because of a business emergency that had arisen in West Germany, leaving her alone to start work on the plant. Even his telephone calls weren't what she had dreamed. He had called her four times in the last two weeks and they had argued three times. That wasn't any way to start a lasting relationship. But both their tempers had had short fuses and they had blamed each other for things that had gone wrong in their work.

"Someone told me once you're always roughest on the people closest to you," Leigh muttered as she stood up and dropped her terrycloth cover-up onto the sand.

She walked to the ocean's edge and let the icy water wash over her feet. It took several moments before she had the nerve to plunge in, but the water's very coldness drove the anger and frustration from her. She knew it was foolish to swim alone, but she was hesitant to ask someone to join her in her peaceful world. She needed to be by herself.

After all, she was a strong swimmer and never went far from shore. She stepped farther into the water until it was lapping about her waist, then turned and let the waves break over her back, letting it massage the tension from her like two hands.

Leigh's brows furrowed as her thoughts turned to Marte, the *other* woman. How important was she to Paulo? She certainly knew everyone at his house. That had been obvious the two times she had visited when Paulo wasn't there. One particular time stuck out in Leigh's mind as especially distasteful, the first time she had seen Marte since returning from the Amazon.

Only three days after their return Leigh had been lounging in a chair by the pool after a hard day working in Paulo's lab. She had felt satisfied with the progress she had made in analyzing the plant. Paulo would be pleased. But when a shadow fell across her and she looked up to see Marte, all pleasure fled her features.

The woman's scowling face glared at her, shocking Leigh with the intensity of her anger. Leigh forced a half smile to her lips and greeted the other woman.

"What are you doing here?" Marte demanded. "I thought you would be long gone by now. Where's Paulo?" Her voice was full of hatred.

Leigh propped herself up on her elbows. "Didn't a servant tell you where Paulo is?"

Marte sat down in the lounge chair next to Leigh's, her narrowed gaze never leaving Leigh's face. "No. I let myself in."

Numb, all Leigh could say was, "Oh."

Her mind began to race with the realization that Marte had a key to Paulo's house. She had known they had been close, but now she knew just how close. Jealousy nibbled at her, but she put a tight rein on that emotion and tried to be friendly.

"Paulo's out of town on business," Leigh said in a neutral voice.

"How long is he supposed to be gone? He was supposed to escort me to a party next weekend."

Leigh could tell that Marte relished disclosing that bit of news and jealousy gripped her firmly. No longer smiling, she answered, "Two weeks. Sorry. You'll have to find another escort. Maybe Jorge is available."

Marte leaned closer to Leigh, fury in her eyes. "I don't think you understand. Let me spell it out for you. *Paulo is mine.* He may amuse himself with other women, but he always comes home to me. If you think it will be any different with you, you're wrong. Other women have stayed in his guest house, but eventually they all left. You'll go, too, when he tires of you."

Rage trembled through Leigh as she rose, every muscle taut with anger. "I don't think our relationship is any of your business. Besides, how could you accept that kind of relationship with a man? I'd think you would want more than the crumbs. If Paulo wanted to marry you, why hasn't he before now?"

"Because I'm no fool. I want Carmen completely out of his system, and that was what the trip to the Amazon was all about. Don't think I'll stand by and let some other woman take over my territory. Those crumbs you speak about are worth millions of dollars."

Leigh hadn't been able to stay there another minute. She had been so angry she wanted to hit Marte. Spinning around, she had fled the terrace and walked briskly toward her car still dressed in her bathing suit. The feel of the wind on her long hair had pushed some of the anger from her, but when she accidentally discovered the deserted beach an hour later she was still furious at Marte—and Paulo.

How had Marte known she was staying at the guest house unless it was a usual practice of Paulo's? Only one person could answer those questions, and Leigh couldn't ask them over the phone. She would have to wait two weeks for answers and she wasn't sure how she could make it through those long days and especially those long nights until Paulo returned.

She shook the disturbing memory from her mind and began to swim, stretching her arms out in front of her in long graceful strokes as the icy water slipped over her.

When she emerged from the cold ocean she felt better, refreshed as she always felt when she managed to escape her demanding work schedule. But since Paulo was returning today, her schedule might change. She wasn't sure how, but she sensed that everything was about to change.

Excitement rose in her as she knelt on the sand and

ran a towel over her body, then rubbed her hair until it was only damp. All her waiting would be over tonight when she saw Paulo and got some answers. But would they be answers she wanted to hear?

"I won't beg for his love," she vowed in the silence of the car as she drove toward his estate. "I'll at least walk away with my pride."

But not her heart. That she knew she would leave in Rio. Paulo had stolen it weeks ago. And she didn't think it would ever be hers again to give.

After stopping briefly at the guest house to shower and change into a red sundress, Leigh walked up to the main house. Paulo had told her not to bother to pick him up at the airport for he had to stop by the office before coming home. She had been disappointed, but they would have the whole evening alone together to get things straightened out. That thought had kept her from insisting on meeting his plane.

As she opened the front door and entered the house, she glanced at her watch, noting she only had an hour more to wait. He had said he would be there for dinner and she had planned a quiet meal for two on the terrace overlooking the rose garden. She smiled as she remembered going over the menu painstakingly with the cook to make sure everything was perfect for their romantic dinner in the moonlight.

The minutes crawled by as she paced from one end of the living room to the other. Every five minutes she found herself checking her watch again. The hour seemed an eternity as she tried but failed to press her doubts to the dark recesses of her mind. Twisting her hands together, she wore a path in the thick carpet. When she heard the front door opening, she froze for an instant, then hurried from the room. It had to be him!

Nothing had prepared her for the scene that greeted her in the entrance hall. She should have known better, but she hadn't. There, standing next to Paulo with her arm tucked possessively through his, was Marte, a sugar-sweet smile plastered on her face. She wore a daringly low-cut dress that left little to the imagination, and a triumphant look glittered in her eyes.

If Paulo were expecting Leigh to fling herself into his arms and rain kisses on his face, he had another think coming, she declared to herself.

He shook loose of Marte's hold and with long strides covered the distance between Leigh and himself, gathering her into his embrace and pressing a hard kiss on her mouth. Her head swam with suppressed desire suddenly released from the tight restraints of the last few weeks. She found herself wrapping her arms about him when moments before she had decided to remain cool and unresponsive. He made her forget all her earlier resolutions with just one kiss that melted the wall of stone around her heart.

The sound of Marte's high heels striking the marble floor brought Leigh back to the real world and she pulled away. Looking at Paulo for the first time in weeks, she saw tired lines about his eyes and mouth that spoke of the long business meetings he had had to attend. The usual sparkle in his dark eyes was gone.

"Well, now that you two have greeted each other," Marte interrupted, "Paulo, we have some things we need to discuss."

Paulo's gaze drilled into Leigh for another minute before he dragged it away and turned to Marte, saying, "Of course, Marte. I'll be with you in a moment. Why don't you go into the study?"

Marte's smile faded slightly as she looked from Paulo to Leigh then back to Paulo. Without a word she turned sharply and headed across the foyer.

When she was gone, Leigh said, "I wanted to pick you up at the airport." She couldn't keep the accusing tone from her voice as a frown slid across her features.

"Someone from the office was supposed to pick me up, but Marte volunteered when she was there this morning. I had no control over the situation, Leigh."

The sharp edge to his voice made her move away a step and she noted the narrowing of his gaze as anger flickered in his eyes. "Don't you understand, Paulo, that . . ."

"Right now I'm too tired to understand your nagging. What difference does it make who picked me up? Marte is a friend and has been for years. She was at the downtown office when my assistant was about to leave for the airport and she took his place. That's all. Now let's drop the subject. I have some things to discuss with her. I won't be long." His tone of voice had hardened with each word and the lines around his eyes deepened with weariness.

Leigh stared at Paulo for a long, silent moment, then said, "Fine. Don't keep Marte waiting." She walked toward the living room, Paulo cursing behind her.

As she sank into a chair, she heard the slamming of a door, then nothing. The silence ate at her as she waited for Paulo to return. It seemed everyone else came first, even Marte. Leigh could accept that business had to take priority over her at times, but not Marte. Leigh needed desperately to talk to Paulo tonight and now she might not get the chance. He was too tired and besides, Marte was there. Somehow Leigh knew Marte would turn Leigh's carefully prepared dinner for two into a dinner for three.

Leigh wasn't surprised when Marte accompanied Paulo into the living room after their "little meeting." What had they discussed? Leigh couldn't help but wonder.

One glance at the look of triumph on Marte's face and Leigh knew the answer. But she pasted a bright smile on her face as if nothing in the world was wrong, as if it was perfectly normal for Marte to be there. She wouldn't let Marte have the satisfaction of knowing she had won. Leigh hadn't given up yet.

"Since it's so late, I've asked Marte to join us for dinner," Paulo said as he fixed himself a drink at the bar. "Would you like something, Marte, Leigh?"

Because Leigh was so unsure of where she stood with Paulo, she began to notice little things. Such as the fact that he asked Marte about a drink first. That his eyes held a friendly warmth when he looked at her.

Leigh had never been jealous in her life, but now she was consumed with it as she was forced to listen to Paulo and Marte discussing mutual friends whom Leigh didn't know or incidents that had happened to both of them before Leigh had met Paulo. Marte had engineered the conversation so that Leigh was almost left out completely except when Paulo occasionally included her.

And when they walked out onto the terrace, Leigh could have slapped Marte for saying, "Oh, look what Leigh had planned for the two of you! I'm sorry I upset her plans." There was no apology in her voice, only a taunt that made Leigh seethe with anger.

Calmly Leigh said, "That's fine, Marte. I'm sure there will be plenty of other opportunities for Paulo and me to have dinner *alone* on the terrace."

The "not if I can help it" look that Marte flashed her told Leigh she had scored a point in her favor. With a great deal of satisfaction Leigh allowed Paulo to help her into her chair before he turned to Marte. The perfect gentleman, Leigh thought. She wished he were less of a gentleman where Marte was concerned.

As the maid served the first course of the dinner, Leigh, determined not to be excluded from the conversation, said, "You'll be pleased at the progress that has been made on the plant analysis, Paulo. And the cuttings have taken root."

"That's one thing I didn't have to worry about while in Europe. I knew you'd do a good job, Leigh. We'll go over everything in the morning before I leave for the office."

"How was your trip? Successful?" Leigh asked quickly as she noticed Marte starting to say something.

"I think everything at the plant in Germany has been cleared up. I hope I don't have to return for a while." Excitement sparked in his eyes. "I have too much to attend to here in Rio."

Leigh's smile grew under the warming glow of Paulo's look. She glanced at Marte and was pleased to see the frown that marred her beautiful face. Maybe this evening wouldn't be a disaster after all.

Throughout the meal Marte wormed her way into the conversation, but Leigh didn't care. Not when Paulo was looking at her so warmly. His gaze was reassuring, a promise of intimacies to come.

But Leigh became impatient as they drank their coffee in the living room. Marte lingered over hers and delayed leaving as long as possible. Leigh could even see frustration edge its way into Paulo's eyes as he glanced at his watch several times.

Finally he rose. "Marte, I've had a very tiring day. I'm sure you'll understand. I'll get in touch with you later on what we discussed in the study." His tone dismissed her, giving Marte no choice but to leave.

"Perhaps we can discuss it further over lunch tomorrow or the next day?" she asked as she made her way to the front door.

Leigh observed them from the doorway to the living room. Marte was certainly doing her best. She was using every trick she knew. Would she succeed?

Not if she could help it, Leigh determined.

"I'll call you tomorrow," Paulo said.

When the door finally closed behind Marte, Leigh

exhaled all her pent-up frustrations and put the evening's events from her mind. She had no real hold over Paulo. He wasn't her husband. Complaining about Marte wouldn't be a wise move, she knew instinctively. Not the first night home. Not after a long trip. Leigh had never been a patient person, but she would need a lot of patience in the next few weeks if her relationship with Paulo was to be a lasting one. And suddenly she knew that despite Marte and Carmen she wanted it to last. She and Paulo might have their differences, but that didn't change the way she felt about him.

Paulo eased down onto the sofa, weariness evident in the droop of his shoulders. Loosening his tie and the top button on his silk shirt, he leaned back and rested his head on a cushion.

Leigh moved softly to the couch. "Here, let me massage your back and neck."

He didn't protest as her hands caressed him. She felt the taut muscles relax beneath her fingertips as he closed his eyes. Just as she thought he had fallen asleep sitting up, he captured one of her hands and brought her around to sit next to him on the couch.

"Enough of that," he whispered before he took her mouth in a burning kiss, tasting, exploring. When he pulled away slightly, depriving her of the touch of his lips on hers, he murmured in a thick voice, "Not when I've wanted that all evening. All the two weeks I've been gone."

His mouth imprisoned hers again beneath the grinding pressure of his lips that sought to leave his mark on her. Leigh parted her lips in an attempt to meet his kiss, her needs overwhelming her as his tongue gently explored her mouth. She trembled with desire for him, clinging to him to assure herself that he was really there, holding her, whispering words of love in her ear.

Lifting her into his arms, he started for the stairs, his

movement halted halfway up by frantic knocking on the front door. He cursed beneath his breath and deposited Leigh on a step before descending to the foyer.

She had never felt so angry as at that moment when she heard Marte's voice. She had managed to come between Paulo and her again. Leigh moved down the stairs to stand beside him.

Marte's clothes were badly rumpled, her hair in disarray. "I've had an accident right outside your grounds," she explained hastily. "I swerved to miss hitting a dog and ended up in a ditch."

Paulo took her trembling arm and led her inside. She leaned into him for support, but Leigh saw the flash of smugness in her eyes, a brief flicker, but there nonetheless.

Had Marte had the accident on purpose? Would she go that far to disrupt the relationship between Paulo and her? Leigh suddenly shivered at the thought of just how far Marte might go to break them up, to get rid of her competition for Paulo's affection.

chapter 11

LEIGH APPROACHED THE secretary's desk and said, "Mr. Silva is expecting me. Leigh Harris."

"Yes, Dr. Harris. Mr. Silva is still in a business meeting, but he should be through any minute. Please have a seat in his office."

The secretary showed Leigh in, then left her alone. This was the first time she had seen where Paulo worked when he wasn't in his lab at his home. It was a large, spacious room with a beautiful view of Rio behind his huge oak desk. Leigh was drawn toward the view. She looked down on a busy city street, then toward the mountains and the Corcovado. One of the things she liked best about Rio was that you could go up into the mountains or for a swim in the ocean, both pursuits within twenty minutes of each other. What a contrast!

Her thoughts turned to Marte and her so-called accident. Marte had no bruises or scratches to speak of. That had been two days ago, yet Paulo and Leigh hadn't been alone to really talk since that night. After Marte had calmed down, Paulo had driven her home, leaving Leigh to spend a lonely night wondering what the woman was up to now.

The next day there had been no explanation from Paulo except that Marte was fine and that he had had her car towed out of the ditch. After that brief statement, Paulo and Leigh had discussed the plant until he had left for the office, where he had been closeted for one day and night.

Leigh had started to wonder if Paulo was just a figment of her imagination when he had called earlier that morning and asked her to join him for lunch. He had finally gotten everything under control. Now he had time for her, Leigh fumed.

She was jealous of his business. She supposed if she were more secure in his love she wouldn't feel this way, but it was hard not to feel as if she were only there for his entertainment—if he had nothing better to do.

What they needed, she decided, was time to get to know each other. Just when she thought she knew him, something would happen to make her feel she really didn't know him at all. But then did you ever really know another person?

The door opened and Marcus entered Paulo's office. He smiled a welcome. "Hello, Leigh. Paulo's secretary told me you were in here waiting for him. I wanted to thank you again for killing that fer-de-lance." He lowered his lean frame into a chair in front of Paulo's desk. "Well, how do you like Rio so far?"

Leigh was instantly wary. Marcus's voice was too casual. True, he had been less hostile in the jungle after the incident with the snake, but what were his real feelings toward her? She wasn't sure.

"I haven't seen a lot of Rio since I've been working so hard on the analysis of the plant."

Marcus flicked a piece of imaginary lint from his coat and said, "Yes, and Paulo has been away for a few weeks." He looked up, and violet eyes locked with green ones. "I still don't think you're right for Paulo. He needs a woman who will devote her whole life to him just as my sister did. I don't think he'll ever love a woman the way he loved Carmen."

"But Carmen is dead," Leigh replied in a not-quite-steady voice. "Paulo is alive with his whole life ahead of him. What do you want him to do? Be a widower for the rest of his life?"

Marcus stood. "No! But you're not the one for him. If I had to pick a wife for Paulo, Marte is more suited to his life style, his culture. He wants a wife who will be a mother to his children and his wife first and last. You American women are all so concerned about your own identities and your own careers that the American male is losing his masculinity. They are nothing but putty in your hands now. Your families are breaking up."

Placing her hands on her hips, Leigh stared at Marcus, stunned. "Is that what you think? Is that what Paulo thinks?"

"I can't speak for Paulo. But, yes, I think he believes that, too."

"What you really mean is that the male species can no longer dominate the female so easily and that distresses you. What kind of relationship is it when the female has no mind of her own—when she's just an extension of her husband and his thoughts? Where's the stimulation? Where's the excitement when the man's word is law and the female can't break it for fear of upsetting the man?"

"Society runs smoother that way."

"And life is duller, too." Leigh turned her back on him, saying, "Now that I know how you feel, you needn't stay. This is between Paulo and me." She stiffened her spine and waited to hear the door shutting.

Was that how Paulo really felt about women? Surely he wasn't that chauvinistic. If he was, she doubted things would ever work out for them. They would have to talk soon, but she was almost afraid to say anything to him. Her heart told her that Paulo wasn't that cold and domineering, but her head cautioned her to beware. Just moments ago she had said that she didn't really know Paulo. Yes, they were physically attracted to each other, and at times that seemed all that mattered. But for a lasting commitment there had to be more.

She would give herself time to get to know him, to find out what he truly thought about women—about her in particular. She knew she couldn't bombard him with hundreds of questions all at once. It would take time.

"I'll start today at lunch," she whispered to herself and turned from the window just as Paulo entered the office.

"I'm glad you could come, Leigh. Now that I finally have a chance to eat more than a quick sandwich, I hate to eat alone." Paulo covered the distance between them and kissed her lightly on the mouth before placing some papers on his desk.

In a teasing tone Leigh said, "You're not going to arouse my pity, sir. I'm sure you could have found some beautiful woman to drag along with you to lunch."

He rubbed his chin as if in deep thought. "Perhaps. But where would I find one who would keep me on my toes as you do? Since your arrival I can't say my life has been dull."

"Paulo Silva, is that all I am? Someone to relieve the boredom?" Her voice held a lightness in it, but she couldn't help the slight tensing of her muscles as she waited for his answer. *It had begun.*

A twinkle appeared in his dark eyes, making them sparkle with mischief. "Oh, you're much more than that. Didn't you tell me you could cook, provided it wasn't over an open fire? And where would I find such a good botanist who is also beautiful to look at?"

Exasperated at the dancing mockery in his eyes, Leigh said, "I can see that I'm not going to get a serious answer out of you."

"Are there serious questions you want to ask me?" The mockery was gone from his eyes now as he appraised her expression. Slowly, as if he were hesitant to speak his thoughts aloud, he continued. "Somehow I get the impression something's on your mind. I know I haven't had time for you since we've returned from the Amazon, but that will change as soon as I straighten out some things here at the office. Matters always pile up when I'm gone for more than a few days."

"Well, I expect you to set aside a whole day for me. I have a surprise planned and it will take a day of your time."

That dancing gleam captured his eyes again. "What surprise? You can't stand in the middle of my office and tease me with things to come." He took a step closer, seizing her hand and dragging her against his granite-hard chest. "What do you have in store for me . . . that will take a day?"

She smiled with pure enjoyment. "I guess you'll just have to take a day off and find out because that's the only way I'm going to tell you."

One of his fingers trailed down her jaw, then forced her chin up until her eyes met his. As always the touch of his hand on her skin made her weak, her legs like quickly melting ice.

"You drive a hard bargain, Leigh Harris. How does Saturday sound?" His dark gaze seemed to reach out and embrace her.

Leigh's breath caught as she looked into his warm

eyes, blazing with desire for her. As he lowered his mouth to hers, she suddenly wished they weren't in his office. She wanted his arms about her for more than just a few minutes. She wanted to feel more than a few of his kisses on her lips, on her flesh, but this wasn't the time or the place, she told herself.

The intercom on his desk sounding in the stillness pulled them apart as Leigh knew some interruption would, for the moment couldn't last forever. Again she stared out the window as Paulo spoke to his secretary, her gaze taking in the hundreds of people walking along the streets. Her senses were keenly attuned to everything around her, as if Paulo had unlocked them with his kisses. She was open and vulnerable—and thoroughly alive.

The colors of Rio seemed sharper. The lush greenery on the mountains sprinkled with vivid reds, pinks and yellows, and the azure water of the bay dominated her sense of sight. Her sense of smell acknowledged the odors of tobacco and the clean fresh scent of the heavy, sultry air of Rio. As Paulo moved toward her, his intoxicating male scent invaded and mingled with the other odors and she swung around to face him.

"That was Jorge on the phone. He wants us to attend a party Saturday night at his apartment."

"What did you tell him?"

"Why, yes, of course."

"But I thought Saturday was my day. Why didn't you ask me?"

Paulo's brow wrinkled into a frown. "You and Jorge are good friends. I thought you would want to go."

"That's not the point. I just want to be consulted about plans that involve me."

"Are we going to start that argument again? I'm going to Jorge's. If you want to stay home, then that's fine with me." He turned abruptly and walked toward the door.

How could she argue with him? He was always walking away from her. Was he shutting her out already? He didn't fight fairly! He didn't give her a chance to speak her mind!

In a terse, clipped voice Paulo said over his shoulder halfway to the door, "Is the Confeitaria Colombo all right with you for lunch? I wouldn't want to be accused of not consulting you on where you're going to eat."

"You're impossible!"

He turned at the door. "I've been told that before. Well, do you want to eat there or somewhere else?"

With a deep sigh Leigh crossed the office and said, "That would be fine."

"Is it all right if I hold the door open for you, or should I go out first and let you follow? I wouldn't want to do the wrong thing."

"Funny." Leigh reached for the knob and yanked the door open, leaving the office without looking back at him.

Men! Paulo was so pigheaded, so arrogant. . . .

A hand grasped her elbow and sent a wave of electricity through her in a flash that unnerved her. She was forced to slow her hurried pace, and couldn't help saying in a sarcastic tone, "What's the matter? Can't you keep up with me?"

A cool smile found its way to his lips. "I didn't know this was a contest. I just didn't see any need to rush to lunch. Is there one?" An eyebrow rose in mockery as his lazy gaze searched her features.

"You mean you have more than thirty minutes to eat?" She was sure Paulo knew very well why she was angry and was trying to make things as difficult as possible. She *wasn't* going to let him get under her skin—well, at least not any more than he had already—which was a lot, she had to admit.

"I have more than thirty minutes," Paulo answered

in a calm, controlled voice. "But I don't relish retracing my steps." As a puzzled look slid over her features, Paulo continued, waving his hand toward a door, "Since this is the restaurant, I suggest we stop and enter. That is, if I'm permitted to make such a suggestion."

This was ridiculous. They were arguing over little things. How would she really get to know him if they couldn't say a civil word to each other? Was she being too sensitive because of what Marcus had said? Perhaps, she acknowledged to herself.

Suddenly a smile dissolved the frown that had captured Leigh's features. Tucking her arm through Paulo's, she said, "Lead the way. You know where we're going, I don't."

A surprised expression touched his eyes for a brief moment before he, too, smiled, a rakish grin that turned her muscles to jelly. Not here! How could she sit through a whole meal looking at him? And the Brazilians didn't like to rush their meals!

They were seated on the top level of the Confeitaria Colombo near the wrought-iron railing where they could look down onto the first-floor diners. Leigh loved the turn-of-the-century setting and the hubbub of business-men talking and enjoying their meals. As she scanned the large open room, her eyes rested on a beautiful stained-glass window in the ceiling.

"Do you eat here often?" She asked after ordering.

"At least once a week. The food's good. This type of atmosphere is rare in Rio. Everywhere I look, a mod-ern building is replacing the old. This provides a touch of the past."

"Is the past important to you?"

"My past is what formed me. My country's past is what has made Brazil what it is today. Yes, it's impor-tant, Leigh, if only to help you understand a person or a country's problems."

Leigh wanted to find out about Paulo's past, to learn what had molded him into the man he was today. If she knew what his childhood was like, she might understand him better.

"Have you always lived in Rio?" she asked first.

She tried not to sound like the Spanish Inquisition, but halfway through their lunch, Paulo threw up his hands and said, "Enough! I think you could write a book about me after this meal. Is there a reason for the third degree?"

"It's obvious that the people here at this restaurant haven't heard of the word diet," Leigh said lightly. "There's enough food here to feed another person, if not two."

"It isn't going to work, Leigh. *Why all the questions?*"

"Because I don't know very much about you." She met his intense look, a warmth encircling her throat at the passion-filled stare he sent her.

"Ours hasn't been a relationship under normal circumstances, I must say. The Amazon isn't Rio." His voice grew more serious. "I don't think I've been fair with you, Leigh. You were overwhelmed by me in the jungle. I promise things will be different now that we are in Rio. I don't think I'll have to fly away again on business. Starting today, my dear, you shall see how a romance is supposed to be conducted."

She didn't question him further, preferring to wait and see what he was talking about. It thrilled her not to know, yet she was filled with curiosity. What was on his mind?

She soon found out. Back at the guest house she was changing into a swimming suit to enjoy Paulo's pool, when a knock at the door startled her. Answering it, she was stunned to see a bouquet of orchids in a messenger's hands. Her own hands were trembling as she read the note from Paulo.

When I think of an orchid I think of your beauty.

Your skin is as creamy as the petals and your loving sensitivity is as rare as an orchid in winter. Have dinner with me at the main house tonight?

The orchids' sensuous fragrance filled the air as Leigh read the note again and again. She stared for a long time at Paulo's signature, "Love, Paulo," hoping he really meant those words.

After swimming twenty laps in the pool, Leigh climbed from the water exhausted and toweled herself dry. The late-afternoon sun was still strong, and soon her bathing suit was dry. She sat for a long time taking in the peaceful surroundings of the garden Paulo had designed.

Only a sensitive man could have created such a beautiful garden. Only a man who loved the outdoors as she did could combine hundreds of different plants into one harmonious whole. This was her favorite place on Paulo's estate—by the pool in the middle of his enormous garden, where the air teased her senses with tantalizing scents. She could close her eyes and become lost in this sensual assault, which made her want to forget all her problems. There was no past or future here, only the present. A present filled with vivid colors, delicious fragrances, and soft sounds of water splashing from the waterfall, of birds singing in the trees, of the breeze rustling the palm leaves.

chapter 12

LEIGH TOOK SPECIAL pains to look her best that night. After placing an orchid in her hair from the bouquet Paulo had sent her, she inspected herself in the full-length mirror. The low neckline of her long gown offered the barest glimpse of her breasts while the crepe material fell in soft folds about her shapely legs. She ran her fingers over the green dress, whose simple lines emphasized her petite frame, then turned from the mirror, satisfied she looked her best. Green was her favorite color and this particular shade matched her jade eyes.

It wasn't quite time for Paulo to be home, but she couldn't stay in the guest house another minute. She would wait for him at his house. Maybe he would come home early tonight.

As she walked up the long drive to the main house,

her auburn hair piled on top of her head, the velvet breeze brushed wisps of it onto her neck. The feathery touch reminded her of Paulo teasing the nape of her neck with his lips. It was a delicious feeling that aroused her, causing pinpricks to rise on her flesh.

When she entered the house, she saw that the door to the morning room was open. Paulo might be there, since the door had always been closed whenever she was in the house before. Peering inside the room, however, she found to her disappointment that it was empty. She was about to turn away when her eye caught sight of Carmen's portrait. How could she have forgotten those violet eyes that seemed to be looking right into the viewer's soul? A shiver streaked down her spine as she stepped closer to the picture, her gaze riveted on Carmen's half-smile, which seemed to be saying to the world, "I know a secret that you don't."

Was the secret that Paulo could never love another woman?

The sound of footsteps approaching the room intruded into the quiet, and Leigh whirled to face Paulo as he pushed the door open wider and stepped into the room.

"What are you doing in here?" he asked. Had there been a trace of impatience or anger in his voice? Leigh couldn't tell, for a mask of indifference fell over his features almost immediately.

"I was marveling at the resemblance between Marcus and Carmen."

"They were twins."

Something flickered in the depths of his eyes as he glanced up at the portrait for a brief moment before turning away. Was it sadness? Regret?

"I don't come here much anymore," Paulo said as he left the room.

Following him, Leigh stopped at the door, then turned to survey the morning room. It must have been Carmen's room—the furniture was what she would have picked out, delicate and white with a cool green material for the cushions. There was even a feminine desk in the corner where she had probably sat to write her letters. Marcus must be right if Paulo couldn't even come into this room, a room that must constantly remind him of Carmen. It was one thing to fight for Paulo against someone like Marte. But how could she fight a ghost?

Leigh had only another month to find out before her project was over. She wouldn't stay in Rio after that if Paulo didn't love her. She couldn't. Unlike Marte, she wanted more than crumbs from their relationship.

She found Paulo in the living room mixing himself a drink, his features grim. He loosened his tie and flung his coat over the back of the sofa before sitting down and taking a long sip.

"Did something go wrong at the office?" Leigh asked, inwardly amused at the very wifely question.

"No. I think all the traveling I've done this last month and the long hours of work are catching up with me. Contrary to popular belief at the office, I'm not invincible. Right now I feel very humanly tired."

Leigh placed her hands on his shoulders and started to massage them. "You're tense. Relax. I've been told I'm quite good at this."

Paulo seized her hands and twisted about to look up at her. "Oh, by whom?"

The corners of her mouth lifted slightly in an impish grin. "Jealous? You should be. I think that's why some guys went out with me. I could always work the tension from their shoulder and neck muscles. I've found that's a valuable asset when dating."

"Well, I don't want to see you practicing on anyone but me. The way things are going, I might need your services often."

"I thought you said nothing happened at the office."

"Not at the office."

The finality in his voice told her not to ask any more questions and for once she heeded the warning. She didn't want to ruin this evening with another argument.

As she massaged his shoulders and neck, she felt the tension slowly leaving him. A sigh of contentment escaped his lips as he rested his head on the back cushion, the lines of strain softening in his face.

"You're hired. I could get used to this every night, Leigh."

"That's the idea, sir. Now do you see why I say it's a valuable asset for a woman?"

He patted the sofa cushion next to him. "Come sit here. I can think of another valuable asset a woman should have and you definitely do."

"Oh, the compliments you give me."

Paulo cradled her to him and stroked her upper arm with a light caressing touch. "By the time I get through with you, you're going to be so razzle-dazzled that you're not going to know what hit you."

Leigh listened to his increasing heartbeat, running her fingers up and down his shirt front. "Well, you've certainly made a great start. Those orchids were beautiful. Thank you, Paulo."

"Now, is that any way to properly thank me?" He turned her around to face him, his dark eyes sparkling.

"I don't know what you mean. That's the only way my mother taught me."

The innocent look she sent him brought laughter to his eyes. "Well, then it's about time you learned another way. You know I believe in continuing education for adults."

Leigh traced the line of his jaw to the cleft in his chin. "Oh, you do, sir. What kind of education do you have in mind?"

"This."

He leaned forward, cupping the nape of her neck and entwining his fingers in her hair, pulling her toward him to meet his lips in a soul-searching kiss that left her fighting for her next breath.

"It's hard to look at you and not want to kiss you," he whispered, then settled his mouth over hers again in a crushing demand of desire.

When he pulled away, he cursed beneath his breath. "Damn! It's almost impossible not to want to pick you up right now and carry you upstairs and make mad, passionate love to you. Why are you so irresistible?" He stood and turned to offer her his hand. "Let's eat dinner before I change my mind and go back on a promise I made myself today."

"What promise?" She laced her fingers through his.

"To slow down. Not to take things so fast. You've made me realize that we know little about each other."

She didn't know whether to be touched by this consideration or upset. She didn't really know how Paulo felt about her. Were things going too fast for him? Or did he think they were too fast for her? Worse, did he regret what had happened in the Amazon yet not know how to get out of the relationship?

Paulo brushed his fingers across her forehead. "No frowns tonight. I won't allow it, Leigh." As they walked toward the moonlit terrace, he continued, "I was hoping you would swim with me after dinner. I feel as if all those lavish dinners I had to attend in Germany are taking their toll on my waistline."

Leigh laughed. "Are you searching for a compliment?" She wrapped her arm around his slim waist and added, "I've never seen any man stay in such good shape, in spite of all the fattening foods you eat. What's your secret? Perhaps you should write a diet book. That's the fad in the United States. Ten easy lessons on how to lose weight."

She halted her step for an instant as her gaze took in the beautifully set table for two. There were two lighted candles with sparkling crystal and silver that caught the light. The heavily perfumed air enclosed them in a world of their own. There was no Marte. There was no Carmen. There was just Paulo looking into her eyes with a warmth that radiated throughout her, making her feel wanted, special to him.

As he assisted her into a chair, his own distinctively pleasant odor mingled with the scent of flowers that filled the air like a potent drug. Every nerve ending tingled with awareness as he brushed his lips across the back of her neck before sitting down next to her, so close at the small table that she could feel the heat from his body.

She looked into his face, his features cast in a golden glow by the candles and moonlight. Her thoughts refused to form a coherent pattern as she stared into the dark depths of his eyes. He was such a kind and gentle man at times, yet there was a touch of primitiveness about him, much like the Indians they had visited. His animal magnetism lured her away from any sane paths she could decide upon when he was not present. Her heart told her to grab what happiness she could and to stay as long as he wanted her there. But her mind told her to be cautious, to remember their differences and to take each day at a time.

Paulo stroked the back of her hand with soft, slow caresses. "Tell me about this other man who hurt you so much. Did you break up recently?"

How could she tell him about Frank when he was touching her in such a delicious way? Frank was the farthest thing from her mind at that moment. But seeing the sincerity in his eyes she felt she had to answer. "Yes. A few months ago. He was a professor at the same college I taught at in Kentucky."

She found herself telling Paulo things she had never

discussed with anyone, not even her closest friend, Margaret. His gentle probing made her relax and unburden herself.

"And you're afraid that a man will dominate you as your father did your mother, is that it?" Paulo asked when she was through.

Suddenly she realized why she had rejected Frank's dominance. Paulo had seen it right away. Her father had smothered her mother all their married life until she had finally rebelled one day and left them. At her father's death, however, her mother had come back into Leigh's life, and somehow she had never resented her mother's leaving. She understood what her parents had gone through. She now had a good relationship with her mother, but perhaps the entire experience had influenced her more than she had thought. No matter what the risk, she knew it was never wrong to fight for happiness.

Paulo grasped her hand and brought it to his lips, snapping her out of the past. "Yes," she whispered in answer to his question, her voice trembling at the feel of his lips on her skin.

Suddenly she felt exhausted from her journey into the past and she still didn't know any more about Paulo's past. "What made you become a chemist when you were already going to inherit the family business?" she asked, hoping to learn more about this mysterious man who tormented her as none other had.

Throughout the dinner Paulo told her more about his childhood and his days at the university studying chemistry, something that had fascinated him while working at his father's factory in Rio. She sensed a deep love for his parents in his voice and began to understand the commitment he felt toward finding a way to ease the pain for burn victims. He communicated the great loss he had felt when his father and sister had died and she couldn't help but think about Carmen. Listening to him, she knew he was afraid to love again because of the tremendous pain he'd suffered. Like herself, he was afraid of commitment.

"Life is a gamble, Paulo," she said when silence fell between them. "In order to win you must take a risk."

For a long moment he stared into the blackness of the night as if in deep thought, then slowly he said, "I know. But that doesn't lessen the pain I feel."

Leigh impulsively clasped his hand. If she could have lessened the pain engraved in his features by taking some of it on herself, she would have instantly.

"I'll tell you what," she said. "I'm ready to swim. I think we've waited long enough since eating." She forced lightness into her voice. "Are you ready to be beaten in a race?"

"And what if I win, Leigh? What are we racing for?"

"You name it—within reason, Paulo Silva."

"A kiss."

"That sounds reasonable. I might just lose the race on purpose."

"You won't have a chance, woman. I'll leave you in my wake."

Laughing, they walked toward the cabana. After dressing, Leigh made her way to the side of the pool. Paulo was already in the water swimming laps. She watched his long, graceful strokes, the muscles in his shoulders rippling.

After three more laps he stopped in the shallow end and said, "Are you waiting until I've exhausted myself before joining me?" There was laughter in his voice.

"Oh, I thought I'd let you warm up since I already did earlier. I thought that would be only fair." She dived into the water and surfaced near him. "But if you think you're ready to be beaten, let's go."

"Next you're going to warn me you were on the swim team at your college," Paulo taunted.

"No, I never found time since I was busy working out for the Olympic swim team," she teased him, then duck-dived into the water, letting the coolness envelop her as she headed for the edge of the pool.

They lined up at the side of the pool, Paulo trying to outdo her by saying, "Let me show you my three gold medals when we get through. The breast stroke is my best event."

Laughing, she said, "I'll just bet it is. I would have brought my medals if I had known we were going to compare."

She poised, ready, as Paulo said, "Let's go down and back. On your mark. Get set. Go!"

She shot out like an arrow, a body's length in front of him. Of course she was kidding Paulo about being on the Olympic team, but she was a good swimmer, having been a lifeguard for three summers to earn money for college. She pushed herself as fast as she could and touched the other end of the pool first. She was ahead halfway through the race, but after glancing toward Paulo, she knew he wasn't swimming as fast as he could. As they neared the end he pulled easily ahead of her and won by several feet.

Panting, she hung on to the side of the pool, gulping in air. "Are you ready for your kiss?" she asked between deep breaths.

"Not here," Paulo laughed. "Say, should I chalk that win up to the male species?"

"If you'll remember correctly, Paulo Silva, I admitted you were stronger than I am. Most men are, but that doesn't mean they're smarter."

With that last statement, she dived into the water and swam toward the steps. Men! They just have to relish their victory aloud for everyone to hear. They certainly weren't a modest group. Then, remembering the teasing grin on his face, it dawned on her that he had been trying to rile her. And he had succeeded. Why did she always rise to the bait? Perhaps because she had always been on the defensive with Frank.

Climbing from the water she said, "Let me show you what the female species *can* do."

"How can I resist an invitation like that?" Paulo swam toward the steps with slow, determined strokes.

When he emerged from the water, she opened her arms wide for him and gathered him to her. His mouth claimed hers in a gentle kiss, an almost brotherly caress far different from his other kisses.

When he pulled away, Leigh's gaze held a question within it. She lowered her eyes to the patch of dark hair on his chest and the glistening copper medallion he wore. "Why do you always wear that medallion?" she asked.

A smile relaxed his features. "It wards off evil spirits."

"Who gave it to you? It's so unusual—so beautiful."

"Carmen. She believed in Macumba, and this is the symbol of the god that watches over me." Masking his expression, Paulo started walking toward the cabana.

Puzzlement furrowed her brow. *Carmen!* Whenever he was reminded of her a shutter came down over his features, making it impossible to read his expression. Was Carmen the reason for the restrained kiss?

Then Leigh remembered the promise he had made to himself. She had sensed the tight rein he had placed on his passions as he held her, his heartbeat galloping as fast as hers. This was one promise she felt would be difficult for him to keep, for she definitely knew he wanted her. Was that all, though? If so, would that be enough for her?

chapter 13

SATURDAY AT LAST! She had waited all week for this—
a whole day alone with Paulo! She was beginning to
understand him, and even though she thought it wasn't
possible, her love had grown. He *had* to feel the same
way about her. If he didn't, she wasn't sure what she
would do. To walk away from him would be almost
impossible, yet she knew she couldn't really change a
person; he had to change himself.

With a light step she made her way to the terrace
where they had been eating breakfast for the last few
days. She halted in the living-room doorway and stared
at Paulo, his head bent over a newspaper. She wanted
to marry him. She wanted a lasting commitment from
him. Did he want the same thing? Maybe today some
of the confusion that haunted her would be resolved.

He moved one suntanned hand toward the coffee cup and took a sip. That hand had brought her so much pleasure with its feather-light touch. His sculptured bronze features were set in a bland expression as he scanned the front section of the paper. When these same features formed a smile, her world brightened. He made her feel special when he turned toward her, his eyes deepening with a gleam that told her of his smoldering desire.

As if he had felt her eyes studying him, he twisted around to look at her. He smiled. The day was wonderful! Nothing was going to interfere with it, not even Jorge's party and all the people who would be attending. Even if Marte walked through the door at that moment, Leigh wouldn't be bothered. *Not today!*

A mischievous face stared back at her. "Are you going to stand there all day and gawk, Leigh, or are you going to join me? I can't eat with you staring at me."

Color flooded her cheeks. "I can't understand why not. I'd have thought you would have gotten used to women admiring you by now." She sat next to him and poured herself some coffee. "Something must be happening to me. To think I'm getting used to this *strong* coffee."

"You're becoming Brazilian." There was a softness in his voice that made her look up into his black eyes. She swallowed away the tightness that had seized her throat. Brazilian? Yes, she supposed she was. This place had a way of growing on her until she couldn't even remember what her life was like back in the States. She didn't even miss her home anymore. This exotic place had slowly become home to her. But then, that shouldn't surprise her since Paulo was a part of it.

"I'd offer you a manioc cake, but we're fresh out." His roguish look made her heart skip a beat.

"I don't know if I ever want to see one of those cakes again."

"Why not?" he asked, in mock surprise. "I thought you had grown quite fond of them in the Amazon."

"I think those last few days I even dreamed about them," Leigh said with a laugh. "It's fine to have them occasionally, but morning, noon, and night is a bit much."

As she ate her breakfast of fresh-squeezed orange juice, toast, and coffee, they discussed the progress they were making on the burn drug. Paulo believed that the sought-after jungle plant would do everything he had hoped for when he had first planned the trip into the Amazon.

When the drug finally became a reality, would she feel less threatened by Carmen, Leigh wondered as she finished her toast and drank the last of her coffee. No, she decided. Only Paulo's complete love would make her feel secure.

"Well, woman, I've been wondering all week about the big surprise you have in store for me. Are you going to tell me now?"

"No. Only that you should wear your bathing suit. I'll wait out here while you change."

He got up and stared down at her. "At least I know one more thing than before. It must be around water."

"Oh, no. I thought we would go hiking in the mountains. Or go to the Tijuca forest. You know you've neglected your tour-guide responsibilities."

"I can see you're not going to give in. I'll just have to wait until we get there. You're most exasperating, Leigh Harris. A man should know where he's being taken."

"You catch on fast. Now go and change."

Pouring herself more orange juice, she realized suddenly that all of the juices served here were freshly squeezed, something she had never found time to do in the States. Life in Brazil *was* different. Not as hurried. Dinner was served much later. Her stomach still protested around eight but she was gradually getting used to eating late.

And the effect of the exotic, moisture-filled climate was a pleasant surprise. Her skin felt soft after only a short time here. She rarely used lotion on it anymore.

Leaning back in her chair, she gazed up at a mountain towering behind Paulo's estate. Rio offered both the coolness of the mountains *and* the warmth of the beaches. She could easily get used to this place, she thought, and to Paulo's presence next to her. To his kisses.

She closed her eyes and relished the quiet of the early morning. But Paulo's whisper-soft kiss on her lips sent her bolt upright in the chair, her eyes flying open. He had approached her again in complete silence, much like the jaguar they had seen in the jungle stalking a paca.

"Paulo!" Her heart was drumming against her breasts. "You startled me! Make some noise when you approach me!"

"Does my attire meet with the day's activities?" He stretched his arms wide and slowly turned for her inspection.

Her gaze lingered on the muscular, tanned legs before moving slowly up to his face. "I suppose you have a swimming suit on under those shorts."

He nodded, amusement carved into his features, the grooves at the sides of his mouth deepening as his grin widened.

"Then it's perfect. Let's go. I'm driving."

"A chauffeur and everything," Paulo mocked.

Leigh bowed. "I try my best to please, sir."

Without warning, he seized her wrist and hauled her against his muscled leanness. His breath tickling the nape of her neck, he whispered, "In that case let's stay here."

Desire laced his voice, causing a streak of passion to race through her. "I think you'll like the beach I'm taking you to." Her voice was almost breathless as he worked his fingers down her back, her control quickly fleeing.

"Ah, a beach. I knew I could get more out of you." A teasing note entered his voice. "But, Leigh, beaches in Brazil are crowded. I would prefer to enjoy you in private today."

The magic of his hands caused her to melt against him completely, the words, "Yes, let's stay," on the tip of her tongue.

But before she could speak, he slowly turned her within the circle of his arms and kissed her lightly on the lips. "But perhaps we'd better go. I could use a cold swim in the ocean. Lead the way, Leigh."

When he saw the picnic basket in the back seat of the car, he smiled and said, "I haven't been on a picnic since I was a child. My parents used to take my sister and me on picnics every weekend that my father could get away. Our favorite setting was near Petrópolis in the mountains. I'll have to take you there soon. You'd love it."

Warmed by the knowledge that he wanted to share a special place with her, Leigh headed the car toward *her* beach. The sun felt especially wonderful this morning, the light breeze bringing the fresh smells of nature to her. The landscape they passed was a dazzling kaleidoscope of colors. Everything was going to work out, she just knew it.

After parking her car at the top of the cliff that rose above the beach, she climbed out and faced Paulo. "Is this secluded enough for you? Except for the birds, we're alone. I've come to think of this beach as mine."

"I guess I'll have to tolerate the birds' presence since they were here first." His mouth quirked into a smile.

"Make yourself useful," Leigh laughed as she waved

her hand toward the towels and picnic basket in the back seat.

"Oh, no way. I thought you believed in women's lib. You'll carry half, too." Paulo reached into the back seat and took half of the stuff.

"I'm becoming Brazilian and you're becoming American. Will we ever get together?"

The suggestive male look he threw her over his shoulder told her yes. Physically yes. But what about mentally, emotionally, Leigh wondered.

After spreading their towels on the sand Paulo suggested a swim, then grasped her hand and pulled her along behind him toward the ocean before she could even catch her breath. He hauled her out into the water until it came up to her waist.

Shivering from the cold, she protested, "Paulo, it's freezing. I'm not used to this water, unlike you Brazilians."

As usual, nothing seemed to bother him. He stood in the icy water as if it were as warm as a baby's bath, his arms folded across his chest and his legs braced apart as wave upon wave pounded onto his chest.

"I thought you said you were becoming Brazilian. I just took it for granted you *were* used to our water. You're not?" One of his eyebrows rose and a devilish glint sparked his eyes. "After all, this is *your* place."

"I like a pool to be heated even in the summer."

But slowly her skin was becoming used to the coldness, her legs not feeling as numb as they first had.

"The best way to get used to cold water is to plunge right in. That slow process you use never works. It's sheer torture and it takes too long." In determination Paulo moved toward her, his intent clear.

Leigh backed away from him. "Paulo, you wouldn't." The pleading tone in her voice didn't halt his progress.

As she was about to whirl and flee to the safety of

the beach, he grabbed her arm with lightning quickness and pulled her against him. He picked her up and carried her a few feet farther out into the ocean, then dumped her into the freezing water.

She came up gasping, the coldness robbing her lungs of air. Gagging on the salt water that burned its way down her throat, she looked up into Paulo's laughing face.

"So you like to play games," she spluttered.

His laughter increased until tears of mirth ran down his face. He was so overcome with laughter, in fact, that he didn't see Leigh move toward him until it was too late. She gripped his legs and pulled, throwing him off balance. He flew back into the water, his face registering surprise as the ocean engulfed him.

Leigh didn't wait for him to regain his footing. That would be dangerous she decided, and headed quickly for the beach, running toward their towels. Paulo wasn't far behind her, closing the gap between them. Just as she was about to reach her towel, he tackled her. They tumbled to the soft sand and rolled over until he had her imprisoned beneath him. He spread her arms above her head and pinned them to the beach.

"You certainly are a brave woman," he said, the menace of his words lessened by the sparkle of desire in his eyes.

"You started it. You got what you deserved."

"You might sing a different tune when I get through with you, Leigh Harris."

Wiggling, she tried to break away from him, but he was too strong. "It won't work, Leigh. You're at my mercy. Now, what should I do to you to make you pay for that stunt?" The sparkle brightened as his passion grew.

Slowly, ever so slowly, his mouth approached hers. She ran her tongue over her suddenly dry lips, which tingled with anticipation. His kisses always made her forget everything but him. When his mouth was only an inch from hers, he halted, his breath brushing her lips like the wings of a hummingbird. Her anticipation became almost unbearable as she waited for his possession.

But instead of kissing her, he jumped up, freeing her, walked toward their towels. An ache filled her with the denial of his mouth on hers. She clenched her hands and pushed herself to a standing position.

"Paulo Silva, if you think you're going to get away with that, you're wrong."

He looked at her in pure innocence. "Get away with what, baby?"

"You're a tease!" Her frustration was evident in her rigid stance as she towered over his lounging figure.

He crossed his arms behind his head and lay back, his eyes closed, a picture of relaxation.

She wouldn't let him get away with that! "Paulo, I need your help," she said in a seductive tone. "I can't reach my back to put on my suntan lotion."

He opened one eye, trying to determine if he should help her. Shrugging, he sat up and took the bottle of lotion from her hand.

She rolled onto her stomach and unfastened her bathing-suit top. "I'm ready."

At first his hands smoothed the lotion over her skin in a businesslike manner, but very quickly their movements slowed. He began to massage the lotion into her back. Under the relaxing motion of his fingertips, she felt as if she were drifting aimlessly on a raft in the ocean.

As he turned her over onto her back, she was no longer the seducer but the one being seduced. He cupped her breast, its fullness filling his hand, and moved over it in slow circles, her nipples hardening under his languorous touch. She trembled with her need for him, the need to feel a part of this man she loved so desperately.

This time when his mouth made an unhurried descent toward hers, their lips touched, his tongue parting her lips to seek the sweetness within. The impact of his sexual arousal ripped the breath from her lungs as his hands played over her flesh, heating her blood to a boiling point.

From far away a sound seeped into their world, a sound of people laughing and talking. Paulo tore his lips from hers and raised his head. Cursing, he sat up and helped her fasten her bathing suit, for her hands were shaking so much she wasn't able to manage it on her own.

With a half-smile, he said, "Well, so much for this being *your* secret place." His casually worded statement was at war with the blazing intensity in his look.

It took Leigh a long moment to regain enough composure to speak normally. "I knew it was too lovely not to be known. I guess I've been lucky in the past not to have shared this beach with other people." Words now tumbled from her mouth to fill the silence that hung between them, anything to take their minds off what could have been. "I packed a delicious lunch. Are you hungry?"

"Yes, but not for food, Leigh. Let's go home."

She rose without a word. In silence they gathered up their towels and the picnic basket, and made their way back to Paulo's estate. The minute they entered the house, though, an excited maid rushed toward Paulo and started chattering rapidly in Portuguese. Leigh couldn't follow all that she was saying, but it was something about an explosion at the Santos plant.

Worry slashed deep lines into Paulo's face. "There's been an accident and I must fly to Santos right away." A distant look appeared in his eyes as if his mind were already racing with things that had to be done.

"Can I come with you? Maybe I can help."

"No. I'd feel better if you'd stay here." He brushed his lips across hers then headed for the stairs. "Maybe I won't be gone long. Let's hope it isn't bad. Call Jorge and see if he can pick you up for the party. You shouldn't stay here by yourself tonight. Go to the party and enjoy it for me." He was halfway up the stairs by the time he had finished issuing his instructions.

The maid scurried away, leaving Leigh standing alone in the middle of the foyer. She didn't want Paulo to go to Santos. She wanted him to stay with her, to hold her, to love her. Just as she thought they were getting close, something always happened. Would they ever be really close to one another?

Shrugging away her disappointment, she made her way to his bedroom to help him pack. The sooner he saw to the emergency, the faster he could come home—to her, she hoped.

She added an extra change of clothes for him while he showered and dressed. Sitting on his king-size bed, she waited for him to finish getting ready, watching his every movement as if she would never see him again.

When it was time for him to leave, he walked over to her and held out his hands. She rose from the bed, melting into his embrace.

"Leigh, I'm sorry about this. I won't be gone any longer than necessary." He framed her face with his powerful hands and stared at her for a long moment as if he were committing her features to memory.

"I know," she whispered just before he touched her lips in a passionate kiss that left his claim on her.

The gentle pressure increased as something ignited between them and fired their blood. Drawing his mouth slightly away, he rained kisses on her face, then hugged her to him in a crushing embrace.

"Oh, Leigh, it's so hard to leave you," he whispered,

his voice muffled by her hair.

A knock at the door parted them and he picked up his traveling bag. Then he was gone. The silence of the house became unbearable as she stood in the middle of his bedroom, gulping in calming breaths. The house was full of servants, but she felt alone the minute he walked away from her. She needed to be around people tonight—anything to take her mind off this empty ache deep within her.

Perhaps she would call Jorge. A party was just what she needed.

chapter 14

OBSERVING THE ROOM full of people, mostly strangers, Leigh began to doubt the wisdom of coming to Jorge's party alone. When her gaze rested on Marte, she *knew* she should have stayed home and was about to turn to leave when Jorge pulled her into the crowd. By the time he finished presenting her to everyone, she couldn't even remember the name of the last person he had introduced her to. Her thoughts were filled with Paulo and what he was doing at that moment. Would he be home soon? He had left on such a tender note. Would they pick up where they had left off? She prayed they would.

The constant buzz of voices around her crept into her thoughts, making her more certain that she had no business being here without Paulo. What fun was a party if he wasn't there beside her? The gathering was certainly not taking her mind off him. On the contrary, he never left her thoughts. Being in a crowd of strangers—well, practically all were strangers—her mind clung to something familiar. When she saw Jorge pass near her with a blonde on his arm, she thought of the time in the jungle when Paulo had saved her and Jorge from the alligator. Even spying Marte from across the room revived memories of Paulo. But those weren't particularly happy ones.

The noise of the party intensified, and Leigh felt the walls closing in on her. A breath of fresh air was just what she needed. Then she would make her excuses to Jorge. He would understand.

The balcony of Jorge's apartment along the Avenida faced the Copacabana Beach and the silvery moon-drenched ocean. Leaning against the railing, Leigh shook her hair loose and let the warm, silky breeze play with it. The view was breathtaking, the warmth of the velvety night enveloping. This was the stuff romantic dreams were made of, she thought—but not when that special someone was not there.

"I wondered when I would find you alone, Leigh darling." Marte's husky voice troubled the peaceful night.

Leigh slowly turned toward her, lifting her chin a fraction as she met the malicious intent in Marte's gaze.

"I'm afraid I have to disappoint you, Marte. I'm just leaving."

"What's wrong? Your and Paulo's blissful world coming apart so soon? Already starting to come to parties without him? I wish, though, that it had been him instead of you joining us tonight."

Marte's vicious words halted Leigh's progress across the terrace. She whirled to face the other woman.

"You would like that. I'm sorry, though, to inform you that there's nothing wrong between Paulo and me."

"Oh, then is he working late? That's usually the first

sign something is wrong—when a man is constantly away from a woman, working, or so he says. Is that it?" Marte taunted.

Doubt flared within the dark recesses of Leigh's mind. Paulo had been working most of the time since they had returned from the Amazon. She hadn't seen much of him. Maybe . . . No! She wouldn't listen to Marte. That's what she wanted—to break them up.

Leigh squared her shoulders and directed all of her defiance toward Marte. "You won't succeed. I love Paulo, and your little innuendos won't work. If he had wanted you, he would never have looked at me."

"He won't look at you for long. You're there to satisfy a male need, nothing more than that. Why else do you think he keeps Carmen's portrait on the wall? Carmen will always be with him."

Icy numbness paralyzed Leigh. She was barely conscious of Marte brushing past her. Sinking onto a lounge chair, she stared at the glittering stars until her eyes burned. But her mind was blank. Minutes became an hour as she tried to piece together her shattered emotions. Yes, she had always known that Carmen was there between them, but what Marte had said made sense. Leigh had hoped that as Paulo grew to love her, Carmen would become part of his past, where she belonged. But why was the portrait still hanging over the mantel unless he couldn't bear to remove it? And yes, he had been working constantly since their return from the jungle. They rarely saw each other. Even tonight work had come between them. Couldn't someone else have handled the emergency? A president of a company didn't have to do everything, did he? Her mind was crowded with doubts that three words from Paulo could have erased. But he hadn't said them yet. Was his love for Carmen holding him back?

A hand touching her shoulder startled Leigh, and she

jumped, her heart thumping against her ribs like the constant beat of the jungle drums. She looked up into Jorge's smiling face.

"I was wondering where you had wandered off to," he said, sitting down next to her. "This terrace is my favorite place in my apartment. During the day I can watch all the beautiful young ladies on the beach and at night I can woo the same beautiful young ladies under the stars. A perfect bachelor pad, as you Americans say." He slanted a glance at Leigh, his smile changing to worry. "Something's wrong, Leigh. Earlier I saw Marte leaving the terrace, looking . . . smug. Has she been interfering again?"

"Let's just say she's trying to shed some light on Paulo's feelings toward me." Leigh struggled to keep her voice from trembling.

Jorge tossed back his head and laughed. "She professes to know what Paulo is thinking? She's smarter than I thought." He shook his head. "No, Leigh, she doesn't know anything about Paulo. She fancies herself in love with him but all she cares about are his money and his position in society. Paulo already has had a wife like that. I doubt seriously he would want another."

Leigh became alert. "What do you mean a wife like that?"

"Paulo and Carmen didn't marry for love. They were good friends, but it never progressed beyond that. They had grown up together and all their lives they were expected to marry. Neither one of them questioned it. I loved Carmen as everyone who knew her did, but she had her faults, as all of us mere mortals."

He took Leigh's hand, his warmth comforting. "Paulo wanted a family very much, but Carmen didn't. So they were married for years and there were no children. She enjoyed her 'career' as a patroness of the arts and the leading hostess in Rio. I can't say Paulo was unhappy, but I could always tell that there was something missing from their marriage. I don't think he felt his estate was a home. Just a place for him to sleep and for Carmen to give lavish parties that were the talk of Rio."

Leigh let what Jorge had just told her settle in her mind before she asked, "Do you think Paulo loves me, Jorge? I couldn't stay in Rio if he didn't. It would be pure torture to see him with other women or just to see him and not hold him."

Jorge smiled. "Only Paulo can answer that. But I will say that he's never acted this way with anyone else. He's never asked a woman to stay at his estate before. Lately I've thought he's more as he used to be in the old days when he and Carmen were just married. Before her social ambitions got in the way of their marriage. At one time I warned you about Paulo not being capable of loving a woman. I was wrong. I think he is. A hard, cynical shell has surrounded his heart these last few years, but I find that it's rapidly vanishing—because of you, Leigh."

The sounds of the party invaded the terrace as someone opened the sliding glass door. "Jorge, you can't desert your other guests just because you finally persuaded a beautiful woman to see your view."

Jorge turned back to Leigh. "Will you join us?"

She smiled, a weight lifting from her shoulders. "In a minute. Go ahead."

When the quiet enveloped her again, she sat staring at the ocean. Only the moonlight streaking across its rough surface illuminated the water. One barrier between Paulo and her had vanished: Carmen. But there was still another wall, perhaps even higher: their differences in viewpoint. As suddenly as hope had blazed within her over the fact that Carmen wasn't an obstacle to Paulo's love, it died when she thought about his opinion of working women, especially wives. Could she sacrifice part of herself for him? She had worked for years to become a botanist. Could she just throw it away and not regret the loss?

What was she doing? Paulo hadn't even asked her to marry him. There was no reason to worry about a problem until it arose.

Leigh reentered the living room and joined in the talking and laughing, making certain to avoid Marte. Around one o'clock when some of the other guests were planning to continue the party at a disco around the corner, Leigh decided to go home, not wanting to party as so many people in Rio loved to do to all hours of the night. The uncertainty of the last month had taken its toll, and she was tired. The mental war that raged inside her made her limbs feel like lead. All her thoughts focused on the soft bed that awaited her back at Paulo's guest house.

When she started to unlock the door to the guest house, it gave way under the pressure of her hand before she had turned the key. She had locked it, hadn't she? A frown drew her mouth into a tight line. Cautiously she inched the door open and peered into the living area. Relief flooded her and she threw the door open wide when she saw Paulo lying on the couch, his eyes closed in sleep. She quietly shut the door and tiptoed over to where he lay.

Her heart caught at the gentle expression on his face, a face full of tenderness, a face without a worry or a concern. The hardness around his mouth was gone. The faintly cynical lines carved into his features were softened, but still aggressively masculine. Looking at him with all her love written on her face, she realized that she had never really loved Frank. Yes, she had been attracted to him. Older by ten years, he had been a wonderful teacher. But she had never felt this radiant glow of ecstasy within her when she thought of Frank. Only

Paulo could mesmerize her with his deep, resonant voice or hold her magnetically with his intense, smoldering gaze that burned into the depths of her being with a relentless force.

A lock of his black hair had escaped onto his forehead and she brushed it back before her lips closed over his own and awakened him. His arms shot out and brought her down on top of him. Laughing, she teased the corners of his mouth before planting a firm kiss on it.

"And to what do I owe this pleasure?" she asked between kisses.

"You're bewitching, do you know?"

She moved her head from side to side slowly, her eyes wide in mock disbelief. "Me?"

The laugh lines at the corners of his eyes deepened. "Yes, you! Never before have I delegated my responsibility to anyone else, but I couldn't keep my mind on what I was supposed to do, so I told Miguel to handle the emergency. I knew I wouldn't be any good until I held you again and made love to you." His mouth ravished hers in a long, sensuous kiss that robbed her of all coherent thought. "When I left, we had some unfinished business to discuss—or rather to—"

His sentence remained unfinished as she smothered his next words with her mouth. Her tongue moved inside his mouth, teasing, tasting.

"Bewitching is too mild a word," he murmured as he blazed a trail of kisses to her ear. He nibbled her earlobe until she was quivering beneath his hands, her senses vibrating with her longing for him.

The ache in the pit of her stomach grew until she thought she would explode from wanting him. His caressing hands were wreaking havoc with her senses as his fingers fumbled to unzip her dress, then to brush down her spine in feather-soft strokes that seemed to turn her bones to water.

Before she realized what was happening, so dazzled was she by the exquisite feel of his hands and lips upon her flesh, she was cradled in his strong arms and he was striding toward the bedroom. His mouth didn't cease its possession of hers as he lay her gently on the bed.

But when he pulled away from their embrace, a coldness struck her. She felt incomplete without his arms around her, his lips on hers. She turned a beseeching gaze on him, silently conveying her need for him. He *had* to end this agony soon!

She watched him shed his clothing, almost tearing off his shirt when a button wouldn't unfasten as quickly as he wished. A laugh bubbled from her throat at his impatience. The same impatience gnawed within her.

She started to rise to undress when he halted her with a hand on her shoulder. She looked into his desire-filled gaze and shuddered from its intensity.

"No. Let me, Leigh." His soft words flowed over her, filling her body with a glow of contentment.

The almost physical possession of his gaze was nearly her undoing. He knelt on the bed beside her and tenderly slid the dress from her shoulders, slowly down the length of her body, then tossed it aside. His searing gaze never left her face as he did the same with her slip, his hands traveling over her skin as if he were blind and trying to perceive how she looked from the feel of her.

A tremor of pure pleasure bolted through her when his hands unclasped her bra, then cupped her breast. With a slow circular motion his thumb and forefinger teased her nipple taut, then he flicked his tongue over it. A moan escaped her lips.

Drawing back, he slipped his fingers beneath the waistband of her panties and slid them off her. His gaze wandered down the length of her, then traveled back to her face, devouring her wherever his eyes roamed. Mind-shattering passion leaped up between them like a living flame that could never be extinguished.

Her breathing came in quick, shallow gasps as his lips tormented the sensitive flesh of her neck, then moved lower to tantalize her breasts. Startling waves of pleasure coursed continuously through her like waves pounding on a beach, one after another, unrelenting.

As her mind floated toward the clouds, she knew this was where she belonged *always*. Paulo was her other half. And as a swirling velvet mist of sensations cloaked them, she dismissed all doubt about their future.

Long ago Leigh's breathing had returned to normal, her heartbeat had slowed to its regular pace as she lay nestled against Paulo's hard body. He caressed her shoulder with his fingertips as they embraced in silence.

"Leigh." He whispered her name as if he were afraid to destroy with words the precious moment they had shared. He tightened his arms around her. "Will you marry me?"

Her heart soared as he spoke those simple, wonderful words. A hot ache in her throat caused the word "Yes" to sound breathless, husky.

Then he was on his side pulling her against his chest as his lips settled over hers in a kiss that branded her heart and soul with his total possession.

chapter 15

BRIGHT SUNLIGHT BATHED the room in warmth as Leigh
stirred beside Paulo. She propped herself up on an elbow
and stared down at his sleeping form, a sheet thrown
carelessly over his hips. She loved every detail of his
powerful male body. Her gaze lingered on the finely
chiseled lips that had explored her body and teased her
flesh until she had cried out in the night for him to finally
end her torment. She could remember combing her fingers through the black thickness of his hair, soft as silk
beneath her fingertips.

What she would never forget was his asking her to
marry him. She had known there was a strong physical
tie between them and now she knew . . .

But he hadn't said he loved her.

Suddenly all her doubts resurfaced to infest her mind

again in full force. She knew he desired her, but *did he love her?*

This doubting everything he did or said was crazy, but Frank had made her mistrust men and their actions. Didn't Paulo's actions say he loved her? Yes—but she wanted to hear those words out loud.

Slipping from bed, Leigh turned on the shower and stepped into the stall. The water pounded her skin, massaging her like hundreds of tiny hands. Closing her eyes, she relaxed under its warmth, letting it hammer at her as if its intensity would erase the doubt from her mind.

Suddenly a cold blast of air struck her and she opened her eyes to see Paulo standing in the doorway, naked, a lazy, sensual look in his eyes.

"I think you have the right idea," he said as his gaze continued to make a bold inventory of her face and body, the desire in his eyes making her feel weak.

"Then join me and shut the door before I freeze," she said with a laugh. She handed him the soap and added, "Make yourself useful. Unless you think I should do half the job."

A twinkle told her otherwise. "No. I'll settle for you returning the favor. I wouldn't want you to go against your women's-lib ideals."

"Oh, never that!" she teased, turning her back to him.

But he had other ideas. He spun her around to face him and slowly soaped her front, his hands lingering on her breasts as they massaged the soap into her skin. When he moved to her legs she was quivering violently. If it hadn't been for her tight grip on the wall handle, she was sure she would have collapsed completely.

By the time he was through washing her, she was frozen by the sensuous feel of his hands sliding over her skin. It took several seconds to realize what he wanted her to do when he held the soap out for her.

His laughter sobered her and she took the soap. As slowly as he had washed her, she glided her hands over the rough texture of his sun-bronzed skin, marveling at the tautness of his flat stomach, at the powerful expanse of his broad chest, and at the muscular legs covered with black hair. She entwined her fingers in the hair on his chest, teasing him with her light touch. She could feel him trembling beneath her fingertips, his heart thumping against his chest, the tempo of its beat increasing with each caress.

The minute the soap was rinsed from their bodies, Paulo reached around Leigh and turned off the water. He scooped her up into his arms and carried her to the bed. Their wet bodies met and came together in a union that fulfilled her aching need for him. . . .

Rolling away from him, Leigh laughed. "Just look at these wet sheets, Paulo Silva. Are you going to help me change the bed since you're responsible for not waiting until we were at least dried off?" She shook her head and clicked her tongue. "Such impatience."

He grasped her wrist before she completely escaped him and pulled her back onto the damp sheets. "I didn't hear you complaining." He nuzzled her neck, nibbling at the soft skin under her ear. "Get your bathing suit on. After breakfast we'll go swimming."

Looking sideways at him, she said in a saucy voice, "Only if you promise not to dunk me."

"And take all my fun away?"

She stood her ground, folding her arms against her breasts. "I won't budge from this spot until you promise. You nearly drowned me yesterday."

"Frankly, my dear, this wouldn't be a bad place to spend the rest of the day if my stomach weren't grumbling so much. I didn't even get to eat dinner last night. I was so eager to get home to you that I forgot."

"Then promise."

"Yes." He kissed her on the lips, then scooted her from the bed.

They were seated on the terrace eating a big breakfast when Paulo broke the silence by announcing, "We'll be married next Saturday and have the reception here in the gardens. I'll let my housekeeper make all the arrangements." His voice indicated that the matter was firmly settled.

Anger touched her. "Don't I have a say in the matter?"

"I don't see any reason for us to wait." A trace of coldness was in his voice as he looked at her frowning face. "I'll take care of everything. You just sit back and enjoy it."

Her doubts returned. "But, Paulo, I want to do something. It is *my* wedding, too. Or had you forgotten?"

"No, Leigh, I hadn't." His cold voice chilled her. "Why are you making an issue out of this?"

"Paulo, I want to work after we are married." There, it was out in the open. They would have to face their differences now, not after they were married.

"Why? You'll be too busy being my wife—and mother to my children."

"Ah, yes. I'd forgotten that you think that's all a woman is good for." Her anger boiled. "I can still work and be a wife and mother, too. I've worked hard to become a botanist. I went to school for six years to accomplish it, and I can't throw away those years just because my husband thinks I should."

"And what I think doesn't count?"

"Of course your opinion counts, but can't we compromise? I could work part-time. You'll see it won't interfere, Paulo."

A forbidding look crept over his features as his mouth twisted into a savage frown. "No!"

Leigh shot to her feet. "Then maybe we should re-

consider this wedding you have planned without my assistance."

She whirled and ran from the terrace, tears welling
up inside her. If she had hoped he would try to stop her,
she was disappointed.

Reaching the guest house, the tears now streaming
down her face, she knew she had to think. But not there
where everything reminded her of Paulo or where she
might see him. She never thought coherently when he
was around, and this was one time she needed to think
straight. Her whole future and happiness depended on
it.

The beach! She would go there.

In minutes she was heading toward the private beach
she had come to think of as hers. When her vision became
blinded by tears, she dashed them away. She would allow
no tears. Right now she needed to think rationally.

On the beach she sighed in relief when she saw that
there was no one else in sight. She had to be completely
alone.

She sank onto the sand and stared at the water as wave
after wave crashed onto the shore. Her mind was blank
as if it had suffered a shock and was now numb.

"What am I going to do?" she finally whispered. The
words caught on the breeze and were whisked away.
Paulo hadn't pulled any surprises on her. She'd known
how he felt. He'd made that perfectly clear the first day
she met him.

A sudden smile touched the corners of her mouth as
she remembered the overbearing, arrogant, pigheaded
man she had faced that first night. But then thoughts of
the tender, gentle man he could be invaded her mind and
chased away memories of that first impression. She loved
both of those men. They were both Paulo! Not just the
tender man but also the arrogant man who was so self-
assured, so commanding that he could run a huge cor-

poration smoothly. Yes, he was opinionated, but then wasn't she, too?

Time seemed to rush by as she went over and over the reasons she should marry him, then the reasons she should return to the United States. What it all really boiled down to was that she felt like half a person without him. If she left, could she survive? He had robbed her of the ability to ever feel complete without him and that frightened her, yet at the same time it made her feel wanted, needed—and loved?

Her head pounded from the intense emotions battling within her. No! She bolted to her feet. The icy water would be a welcome relief from the heat of the sun that beat relentlessly down on her. Perhaps it would even drive those warring factions from her thoughts and she could finally make a decision.

She plunged into the cold surf and attacked the water with hard, even strokes that quickly took her away from the shore. Before she realized it, tall waves were forming, making her progress difficult, and she turned to head back to shore. She had never come out this far and she chided herself for not paying more attention to where she was going. She fought her way toward the beach, waves now breaking over her head, pushing her under. Each time she surfaced gasping for air, another wave would crest and drag her under. As she frantically rose again toward the surface, the strong undertow held her down, refusing to relinquish its hold on her.

She was drowning! How ironic that she should die now, just when life seemed to offer so much and promise so little. Then panic overwhelmed her.

Her lungs burned from the lack of air. Her muscles no longer obeyed her commands to move. Blackness engulfed her....

A noise penetrated the darkness of her mind and pushed her toward consciousness. She felt something touching her, a hard pressure on her mouth and chest. Air flooded her lungs, the burning sensation gone. Her body no longer felt cold but warm as she felt the sun cloak her.

Rolling her head to the side to avoid the intense rays of the sun, she opened her eyes halfway and saw an orchid lying on the sand, its cream-colored petals with streaks of red the most beautiful sight she had ever beheld.

She was alive!

She tried to move, but every muscle ached. She wanted to touch the orchid to reassure herself that she wasn't dreaming, that her foolishness hadn't resulted in her death, but it was too much of an effort.

Then she heard his deep voice and knew everything was all right. Gathering her strength together, she sat up and looked at Paulo, deep lines of worry engraved on his features.

Relief raced over his face as he crushed her to him and planted kisses all over her face. "If anything had happened to you, Leigh, I would never have forgiven myself. I sat and fumed on the terrace for an hour until I decided you were more important to me than *anything*. I knew I couldn't lose you, and if working part-time was what you wanted, then that was fine with me." He pulled back and stared down into her face, his eyes misty. "I wouldn't be happy without you, and I couldn't be happy if you weren't. *I love you, Leigh.*"

"I love you, Paulo." She brought his head down until their lips met in a kiss that committed them to each other forever.

He pulled her closer and lay her head on his shoulder. "I saw you trying to get back in to shore. The waves are bigger than usual today, Leigh, but even on a normal day the ocean can be dangerous in Rio."

"I know. I'm a strong swimmer and I never went very

far from shore before. Today I tried to escape my problems by concentrating on swimming. I didn't even pay attention to where I was going. I just wanted to swim forever until I was too exhausted to have to think of a solution to our problem." She turned to look into his face, running her finger down his jawline. "I want to work for a while. At least until we begin a family. Then when the children start school, I might like to go back to work. I'm not the type of woman who can stay home and just keep house. I have to have something to challenge me. Do you understand at all, Paulo?"

The smile he gave her wrapped her in the security of his love. "I'm beginning to. I won't mislead you and let you think it will be smooth sailing for us from now on, that suddenly we will agree on everything. But then that's what makes life interesting. I know I'm stubborn and opinionated, but you have a way of making me see your side. I *am* a fair man."

Still sore and exhausted, she rested her head on his shoulder, contentment flowing through her, a feeling that only Paulo's love could give her. From the corner of her eye she saw the orchid again and picked it up.

"A gift, Leigh. When I realized you meant more to me than all my views put together, I knew I had to find you. I went to the guest house and noticed the car was gone. Then I knew where you were. Your secret beach. This was my peace offering." He brushed his finger over a petal, then took the flower from Leigh and placed it behind her ear.

He combed his fingers through the silken fire of her hair and framed her face with his hands, pressing his lips to hers. "Let's go home, Leigh," he murmured against her mouth, caressing the word "home" as if it were a special place to him—a place where they would be a family.

Nestled in his arms, Leigh felt complete and whole. "Yes, I'd like to go home," she agreed quietly as the fragrance of the orchid drifted over her and she touched it gently.

Second Chance at Love ™

Please turn
the page
for our questionnaire
and an exciting
SECOND CHANCE

AT LOVE
offer!!!

QUESTIONNAIRE

1. How many romances do you buy each month
   - ☐ 5 or less
   - ☐ 5 to 10
   - ☐ more than 10

2. Do you like, primarily
   - ☐ modern-day romances
   - ☐ Regency period romances
   - ☐ both, equally
   - ☐ other historical romances

3. Were the love scenes in this novel
   - ☐ too explicit
   - ☐ not explicit enough
   - ☐ handled tastefully

4. Do you prefer stories set
   - ☐ in the USA
   - ☐ in foreign countries
   - ☐ both, equally

5. How old do you like your heroines to be
   - ☐ 17 to 22
   - ☐ 23 to 27
   - ☐ 28 to 32
   - ☐ 33 to 40
   - ☐ over 40

6. The length of this book is
   - ☐ too short
   - ☐ just right
   - ☐ too long

7. The main reason I buy a romance is
   - ☐ a friend's recommendation
   - ☐ a bookseller's recommendation
   - ☐ because of the cover
   - ☐ other reason:_____

8. Where did you buy this book?
   - ☐ chain store (drug, department, etc.)
   - ☐ bookstore
   - ☐ supermarket
   - ☐ other:_____

9. Mind telling your age?
   Our lips are sealed…
   - ☐ under 18
   - ☐ 18 to 30
   - ☐ 31 to 45
   - ☐ over 45

10. Check here if you would like to
    - ☐ receive the SECOND CHANCE AT LOVE Newsletter

· ·

Fill-in your name and address below:

name:_____

street address:_____

city_____state_____zip_____

Please share your other ideas about romances with us on an additional sheet and attach it securely to this questionnaire.

PLEASE RETURN THIS QUESTIONNAIRE TO:
SECOND CHANCE AT LOVE, THE BERKLEY/JOVE PUBLISHING GROUP
200 Madison Avenue, New York, New York 10016

**WATCH FOR
6 NEW TITLES EVERY MONTH!**

Second Chance at Love™

Dear Reader,
Welcome to the <u>Second Chance at Love</u> circle of readers! The <u>Second Chance at Love</u> romances are written
with *you* in mind. To find out more about you and what
you like, we'd like to ask you to take a few moments and
fill out the questionnaire on the opposite page and return it to us. And, in return, we'll pay for postage on the
Second Chance order you place using the coupon that
follows.

_____ 05703-7 **FLAMENCO NIGHTS** #1 Susanna Collins

_____ 05637-5 **WINTER LOVE SONG** #2
Meredith Kingston

_____ 05624-3 **THE CHADBOURNE LUCK** #3
Lucia Curzon

_____ 05777-0 **OUT OF A DREAM** #4 Jennifer Rose

_____ 05878-5 **GLITTER GIRL** #5 Jocelyn Day

_____ 05863-7 **AN ARTFUL LADY** #6 Sabina Clark

_____ 05694-4 **EMERALD BAY** #7 Winter Ames

_____ 05776-2 **RAPTURE REGAINED** #8
Serena Alexander

_____ 05801-7 **THE CAUTIOUS HEART** #9
Philippa Heywood

_____ 05907-2 **ALOHA YESTERDAY** #10
Meredith Kingston

All of the above titles are $1.75 per copy

Second Chance at Love

All of the above titles are $1.75 per copy

Available at your local bookstore or return this form to:

SECOND CHANCE AT LOVE
The Berkley/Jove Publishing Group
200 Madison Avenue, New York, New York 10016

☐ I've enclosed my completed questionnaire— Publisher will pay the postage.

☐ No questionnaire included. I've enclosed 50¢ for one book, 25¢ each add'l book ($1.25 max). No cash, COD's or stamps. Total amount enclosed: $_____ in check or money order.

NAME_____

ADDRESS_____

CITY_____STATE/ZIP_____

Allow six weeks for delivery.   SK-39